Stolen Time

This story is for all the knitters throughout the world who have yet to meet their Prince Charming . . . and for those lucky enough to have found him.

Stolen Time

Chloé Duval

Translated from the French by
Domitille Vimal du Monteil

LYRICAL PRESS
Kensington Publishing Corp.
www.kensingtonbooks.com

LYRICAL PRESS BOOKS are published by

Kensington Publishing Corp.
119 West 40th Street
New York, NY 10018

Le Temps Volé by Chloé Duval © Bragelonne 2015
Translated from French by Domitille Vimal du Monteil © Bragelonne 2016

All Kensington titles, imprints, and distributed lines are available at special quantity discounts for bulk purchases for sales promotion, premiums, fundraising, educational, or institutional use.

Special book excerpts or customized printings can also be created to fit specific needs. For details, write or phone the office of the Kensington Sales Manager: Kensington Publishing Corp., 119 West 40th Street, New York, NY 10018. Attn. Sales Department. Phone: 1-800-221-2647.

Lyrical Press and Lyrical Press logo Reg. U.S. Pat. & TM Off.

First Electronic Edition: June 2017
eISBN-13: 978-1-5161-0088-0
eISBN-10: 1-5161-0088-3

First Print Edition: June 2017
ISBN-13: 978-1-5161-0089-7
ISBN-10: 1-5161-0089-1

Printed in the United States of America

Dear Reader,

First of all, I want to thank you for buying this book, *Stolen Time*. The story and its characters have a special place in my heart, and I can't tell you how glad I am to be able to share them with you. I hope you'll love them as much as I do.

Now, as this book takes place in France, I thought I'd fill you in on a few details about the French school system, the *Compagnons,* and a few other things.

In this book, you will meet Flavie Richalet. In her spare time, Flavie is a romance novelist and a knitter, but her first job is to teach history and geography in a public middle school. Let me tell you a bit about how the French school system works: In most French primary, middle, and high schools, pupils go to school all day on Monday, Tuesday, Thursday, and Friday, and in the morning on Wednesday and Saturday. Wednesday and Saturday afternoons and weekday evenings are devoted to homework and extracurricular activities like sports. Clubs don't meet on Sunday, so the pupils stay home to study or spend time with their families.

Contrary to the American system, class appellations work backward from the last high school year, which is called *terminale* (equivalent to the twelfth grade). So after primary school, the first year of middle school is called *sixième* (which means sixth and is equivalent to sixth grade), the second year is *cinquième* (fifth, equivalent to seventh grade), and so on till you reach the *seconde* (second, equivalent to tenth grade), the *première* (first, equivalent to eleventh grade) and the *terminale* (twelfth grade). Flavie teaches pupils from sixth to ninth grades, so from the *sixième* to the *troisième* in the French system. Secondary education establishments are divided into middle schools and high schools. Middle school goes from *sixième* to *troisième* (four years) and high school from *seconde* to *terminale* (three years). Most cities and towns have primary schools and middle schools, but in the country, pupils often have to go to the nearest town to go to high school. When you reach the *terminale* (last year of high school), you graduate with a high school diploma called *bac-*

calauréat, which allows you to go to university. But that's another story.

Another important and lesser known aspect of French culture that my book introduces is the Compagnons du Devoir, a century-old institution that stems from the guilds of the Middle Ages. Its main goal is to train young people to become master craftsmen, such as stonemasons (like my hero), or bakers, landscapers, locksmiths, blacksmiths, etc. The *compagnonnage* is much more than just training for a trade. It's also a way of life. As they train and work, Compagnons live together in a kind of boarding house, administered by a housemother. The Compagnon way of life is one that fosters values like generosity, cooperation, and the pursuit of knowledge. You will learn more about this way of life and how it shaped my hero's character.

Last, but not least, a few key events of my story take place on the famous Bastille Day, the fourteenth of July. On this holiday, every city in France celebrates the Storming of the Bastille, which took place on July 14, 1789—an event that would lead to the French Revolution, and the end of centuries of absolute monarchy and the divine right of kings. On that day, nobody works (except hospitals, firefighters, and all emergency services, of course). Shops and malls, offices and factories are all closed, and cities and towns commemorate the Storming of the Bastille with fireworks and, in many cities, with open-air dances too, sometimes called the firefighters' ball. In Paris, military troops march down the Champs-Elysées to demonstrate the country's fighting power. The air force puts on a beautiful show with blue-white-red smoke. The whole show is broadcast on TV, so many people enjoy watching it from the comfort of their homes.

Some fireworks are truly spectacular and very famous throughout the country, like the ones in La Baule or Nice, displayed on the beach, above the sea, or the one in Paris, displayed on the Champ de Mars, next to the Eiffel Tower.

Contrary to what the Fourth of July represents to the American people, the true meaning of Bastille Day seems to have dimmed in the last decades—even though the celebrations are still very popular and well attended. Nowadays, people enjoy the day off from work, and use the time to do fun activities with the children, or visit with friends, just like they do on any other national holiday.

I hope those few facts will allow you to better delve into the story, and understand the ins and outs of the choices each character has made. Thank you again for reading *Stolen Time*. Don't hesitate to let me know what you thought about the book! I'd love to hear from you!

Happy reading!

Chloé

Prologue

Karouac, Brittany
September 4, 1975

It was the most important day of her life.

She'd been waiting and preparing for this day for weeks, and she should have been deliriously happy. She should have been lighthearted and smiling.

But instead, she felt strange and uncomfortable. As though she was forgetting something important. As though she was about to make a mistake.

It's just apprehension, she told herself. The usual jitters all women feel before they commit for life.

But did all women think of their first love on their wedding day?

Amélie closed her eyes, and Erwan's beautiful face appeared in her mind. She pictured his irresistible smile, his gray-blue gaze, his unruly hair, always too wild to lie flat. She felt his rough hands on her skin, his lips on hers, as though it were only yesterday that they had lain together on the beach.

She shook her head, willing herself to dismiss the memory. It was foolish to think of him, especially right before her wedding. It had been so long ago . . . four years, almost to the day. He'd obviously forgotten her, moved on with his life. He'd never written to her, never phoned her, never gotten in touch with her. She'd waited weeks, months even, for him to reach out to her, before she'd accepted the truth. It had only been a summer fling. So she'd grieved, but then looked to the future. She'd thrown herself into her studies in fashion-design school to forget. Forget all about him.

And now she was finally happy. She'd finished school and gotten the job of her dreams with a small fashion company that appreciated her style and her slightly extravagant ideas. It was almost more than she'd ever expected. Moreover, she was about to marry a wonderful man, one who loved her more than anyone and whom she loved very much. She knew they'd have a great life together.

So why? Why was she thinking of the past, of a painful, best-forgotten period of her life, on the day she was going to marry Paul, for better or for worse?

She took a deep breath, trying to calm her heart, her nerves, her mind. She patted her veil, smoothed a few nonexistent creases in her satin and lace wedding dress. She'd designed it herself, and it was stunning, even if she said so herself. It was the dress of her dreams.

Again, Erwan appeared in her mind's eye.

"For God's sake!" she swore, cutting herself off immediately.

Someone knocked on the door and her mother peered in. "Are you ready, sweetheart?" Viviane Lacombe asked, beaming.

Amélie cast a last glance into the mirror, took a deep breath, and nodded. "I am."

It was no longer time to wonder about the past.

So, she left her home, the home where she grew up, and, lifting the hem of her dress in one hand, her father at her side, her mother in front of her, beaming much more than her daughter was, Amélie slowly walked the short distance to the beautiful church of Karouac, where her parents had been married. Paul was waiting for her there. Her family was waiting for her. The minister, and all their friends, were gathered here today to celebrate her wedding to the love of her life. She couldn't wait to go in and marry Paul, the man who had always been there for her. Who loved her more than anything else. She couldn't wait to start her life. The life she had chosen for herself.

Yet before she walked into the church, she couldn't help stopping to gaze around, searching for a face, a smile. She shook her head and cursed the damn memories trying to spoil the happiest day of her life. She turned back and smiled at her father, took hold of his proffered arm, and waited for her cue.

Hidden in the shade of a porch, unseen, Erwan watched as the love of his life walked into the church on her father's arm to marry another man.

He'd been too late, and he'd lost her once again—forever.

He tamped down the urge to enter the church and beg Amélie, on his knees if need be, to come with him, repeating what he'd written in that unanswered letter four years ago, and walked away, his heart breaking, leaving Karouac behind him.

Once again, and forever.

Chapter 1

T he letter came on a Tuesday.
That sentence alone would make a great title for a novel, although my editor would want it shortened. But I thought it was catchy, to the point, and mysterious. It sparked my imagination. What was in the letter? What was so special about it? Why would someone write a novel about that particular letter?

People write millions of letters every day; well, maybe only thousands now that the digital era has pretty much killed traditional mail. So why the fuss?

Because it wasn't just any other letter.

This one was special. It wasn't an advertisement for the latest shop, it wasn't another annoying scam asking for money. It wasn't a bill either—which is a good thing, because I hate bills as much as I hate phone surveys.

It wasn't any of the above. It was a handwritten letter from one real person to another. From a man to a woman. A man who—

But I'm getting ahead of myself. Let's start at the beginning, shall we?

So the letter came on a Tuesday.

Barring a few details, that day started like any other.

The morning sun shone brightly for the first time after weeks and weeks of endless rain that everyone in Brittany was fed up with. It was May, and to my delight, I'd *finally* slipped into the first sundress of the year. At long last, spring had arrived, bringing with it a fresh breeze of optimism and happiness.

As was—and still is, actually—so often the case, I'd woken up in front of my computer, bleary-eyed from the lack of sleep, still halfway into my characters' minds.

I write love stories—romantic love stories, erotic love stories, and everything in between. I write the books for myself first, because serious teacher though I may be, I still have a soft heart, and I love romantic and emotionally moving stories that come with a happily-ever-after; for my friends second, because it's fun sharing my stories over a couple of rows of moss- or rib stitches; and thirdly for my fans and the readers of the world, because a little romance never killed anyone—and neither did a lot of romance—and our lives are serious enough as they are.

That day, I'd spent most of the night writing—the last four hours, to be precise, which meant my total amount of sleep was much too little for comfort and especially short of the "beauty sleep" mark. But I didn't have anyone to look good for, so who cares?

Still half asleep, I'd headed to the middle school where I taught history and geography. Some light makeup and a business-casual outfit had hidden most of my sleep deprivation, but my brain had had a hard time picking up the pieces. I'd need all my wits and a large amount of tea not to get all my lessons confused.

Because even though they may be adorable (most of the time) and understanding (more or less), there is nothing in the world a student likes better than to be able to tell a teacher she's wrong. And I'd rather avoid that, thank you very much.

So, after a mildly difficult day—I'd taught four classes and marked a heap of homework in my trademark purple pen, the one extravagance I allowed to disrupt my sensible, well-behaved teacher image—I dashed home just long enough to grab my knitting, some cookies I'd baked the day before, and the notebook I always kept in my purse, and headed toward the center of Karouac, the charming little Breton town—complete with narrow cobblestoned streets and half-timbered or gray-stone houses—where I had been living for the last few years. Vic and the others were probably already waiting for me at her shop, Le Fil d'Ariane.

Though infrequent at first, our Tuesday evening knitting meetings had quickly become a regular fixture in my busy week—and something I needed as much as writing or breathing. It was my way of relaxing, of turning off my overwrought brain and imagination. Some people do yoga or martial arts. I knit, and once a week, in rain, shine, or snow—rare though that may be around here—I grabbed my needles and met up with my friends in Karouac's only knitting and sewing shop.

Victoire, the owner, was the "mom" of our group. The shop was her baby, her creation, the symbol of the new life she'd built in spite of the obstacles in her path. She'd opened nearly ten years ago, upon inheriting a tidy sum from her late grandmother. Thirty-two years old and married to a notoriously unfaithful man, Vic had followed her grandmother's advice and reclaimed both her freedom and her maiden name before starting again from scratch. After some difficult times (the joys of living in a small town with some quite busy busybodies), her shop had prospered, becoming the lively, colorful image of its owner, and one we cheerfully invaded every week.

The knitting circle—my preferred nickname for our group—had started with Victoire and Cécile, the oldest member and my first friend in Karouac. For some months after the shop opened, while Vic struggled with bills and a lack of customers, the circle had numbered only two. Vic likes to say that without Cécile's unwavering support, she would probably have given up. It was Cécile who had not only suggested a knitting circle, but also had brought Bérénice and Angélique into the fold, and later myself, once I'd moved to Karouac.

I'll probably be grateful to her for the rest of my life.

The knitting circle is more than friends—it's family. After five years in their company, I couldn't imagine life without them, without their jokes and their advice, and especially not without their unconditional friendship.

They were nearly all there when I breezed in, somewhat disheveled by the unrelenting Breton sea wind—why did I decide to walk here, again?

"Hi, everyone!" I said as the door tinkled shut.

Vic, Cécile, and Bérénice immediately smiled and greeted me. Only Angélique was missing.

"Hi, Flavie!"

"Hello, gorgeous."

"Hi," I repeated. "How're you all doing?"

"Fine, fine!" replied Vic.

"Me too. So, what's up?" asked Cécile.

I dropped into my chair and sighed deeply. "Ladies, the situation is critical. I'm pretty sure my students think I'm an idiot."

As I spoke, I opened the tin of cookies and set it on the table. "Help yourselves. I've brought the dessert."

I took the lead and bit into one of the cookies, trying not to moan with delight. I'd baked Kinder chocolate cookies, which, in my eyes, are the closest you can get to heaven on earth. I wouldn't be surprised to learn they've been banned in some place or other.

"Flavie, you're the best!" Vic exclaimed.

"Great!" Cécile said. "I'm starving."

"So," Bérénice asked in a soft voice while munching on a cookie, "what did your students do this time?"

"They handed in the homework I assigned," I said, my mouth full.

"So far, so good," Bérénice responded.

"I skimmed through it before coming over here, just to get an idea of what to expect. Guess what?"

"They cheated?" Vic guessed.

"And the winner is . . ." I said with a flourish. "They copied the Wikipedia page. Did they seriously think if they added a couple of spelling mistakes I wouldn't notice?"

"All of them?" Bérénice asked, shocked.

"No, but at least three. And you know what annoys me most?"

"I'm guessing we're about to find out," Vic said with a smile.

"Among the three, there's a very smart girl who is perfectly capable of handing in excellent homework! She doesn't need to cheat. The other two are full of big ideas, and they are more of a challenge. But I don't know. I kinda feel like a failure, since I didn't succeed in teaching them the values they're going to need in life."

"Wow, hold your horses, there!" Cécile interjected. "Don't you think you're being a bit hard on yourself? There have always been cheaters. It doesn't mean *you*'re not a good teacher . . . This one isn't on you."

I sighed again. "I don't know, Cess. Sometimes I wonder whether I make a real difference. I feel like I'm not helping them."

"Don't let it get to you, though." Vic was always the most pragmatic of us all. "You can't save the world, you can only teach history and geography. Don't tie yourself into knots. Here, have another cookie." She slid the tin toward me. "Everything looks better with a little sugar in your system."

"Vic's right. Not just about the sugar," Bérénice added with a smile as I selected the largest cookie. Sugar was a way of life for Bérénice. Her cookies, pastries, and cupcakes were the best for miles around. She had her own pastry shop, Les Délices de Bérénice. "You shouldn't take it to heart. You're doing your best, and that's what matters."

"My best isn't enough, unfortunately."

"You're not a social worker. It's not your job to save them." Cécile was emphatic. "Leave the superheroing to people who get paid for it. When I show someone a house, I don't tell them how they should decorate. That's not part of my job."

When she wasn't knitting (for herself, for us, or for the homeless), Cécile was a real estate agent, and had been for years. *Some people help you find your soul mate*, she liked to say, *I help you find a home.* She'd been the one to find the location for Le Fil d'Ariane and Les Délices de Bérénice, as well as my own house. I'd been a fresh-faced graduate when I'd come to Karouac a few years ago, ready to save the world one student at a time, and Cécile had helped me buy the lovely little cottage I lived in today.

"My job," she continued, "is to help people find the home of their dreams. What they do with it is not my concern. Being a teacher is the same. Your role is to give your students the keys to understanding the world so they can make their own decisions. You can't decide for them and solve all their problems."

I wanted to tell Cécile that she might be right—a common occurrence—but it still bothered me that my kids would prefer to waste their brain cells copying from the internet rather than think for themselves. I viewed it as a personal failure.

The doorbell interrupted me, however, and Angélique's entrance meant the conversation would go in another direction, which suited me just fine. For once, I didn't entirely agree with my friends on how far I should be involved in my students' lives, but I was too exhausted to think about it anymore. For now, at least.

The rest of the conversation would have to wait for my brain to reboot.

"Hi, everyone, sorry I'm late!" Angélique apologized as she rushed in.

Angélique was the only member of the circle to be officially "off the market." She had an adorable son, Olivier, whom she occasionally brought with her so we could coo at him with all our might, something we had no trouble doing.

"Hey, Angel." I smiled warmly at her. "What's up? No baby today?"

She sat down and took out her own knitting. "His father's looking after him. How 'bout you? Oh, cookies. Did you make them, Flavie?" I nodded, and she helped herself to one. "You're fabulous, and they are delicious! You really need to give me the recipe. And Bérénice too. You might want to start selling fancy cookies," she added, turning to Bérénice.

"I've been thinking the same thing!" Bérénice answered.

"Angel, you can't even manage pasta," Cécile reminded her, unable to resist teasing Angélique. "Forget about the cookies."

"I wouldn't bake them—Hervé would!"

"I'd been wondering . . ."

"I gave up cooking a long time ago. To be honest, my husband is so sexy working in the kitchen, I don't try very hard. I'd much rather sit with a glass of wine and watch him."

"Never underestimate the appeal of a man with an apron and flour on his hands," Vic intoned solemnly.

"Amen!" Cécile bit into another cookie and turned toward me with an excited expression on her face. "Speaking of men and appeal . . . Flavie, I've been dying to hear the rest of your book. Are Liam and Clarissa together now? Did they speak to each other? Did he tell her who the blonde girl from the other night was? Did they sleep together? Because it's all well and good, but there are priorities in life!"

Liam and Clarissa were the two main characters of the novel I was working on—and the cause for the bags under my eyes.

Bérénice joined in. "Me too. I've been thinking about them all week!"

"Well . . . They talked to each other."

I summarized the latest events, fresh from that morning. They gave me feedback, talking over each other. I loved the moments when we talked about my characters. It was as though they came alive outside my mind and my computer. We talked about them as though they were real people—and most of the time, I almost expected them to step into the shop and take part in the conversation.

"Which is why I've been running on so little sleep," I concluded. "Liam kept me awake all night . . ."

"What happens next? Is it the end?"

"No, I have a lot more planned."

For the next two hours, we switched subjects several times, as we always did, from my novels to our knitting projects, to men, cookies, the latest books we'd read, laughing all the time. We didn't talk about my students again.

Like every Tuesday, time flew by, and after the meeting, we went out for crêpes at one of our favorite haunts. The crêpes were delicious. The owner had a really cute smile and he liked us; he almost always gave us a treat on the house. Who could resist a man like that? Not us, that was for sure, and we almost always stopped by after our meetings.

The sun had set by the time we all left, and I decided to walk home by the beach. Over the five years I'd spent in Karouac, I'd grown to love the seaside. Hidden at the very top of the Pink Granite Coast, Karouac was my own little slice of sand and sea. I'd formed a lot of memories here. The beach was always overcrowded in summer but nearly empty the rest of the year, and I would walk long hours, barefoot, just to feel the sand between my toes, the wind on my face, the salty taste of the sea on my lips and tongue. It was during one of those walks that I had found what would become my favorite spot, a tiny, isolated creek accessible only at low tide. I liked to walk there, to sit and write, or just think about my characters while listening to the sea. It was soothing. Quiet and soothing. The pier, a long arm going into the sea, was another spot where I liked to spend time, sitting on a bench with a travel mug of tea and either my notebook or my knitting, and watch the sun set, seagulls screaming over my head.

Until I graduated from high school, I'd lived all my life in Lannion, which is situated a few kilometers from here; but Karouac, with its five thousand inhabitants, its rural charm and its flower gardens, stole my heart. After five years, I couldn't imagine living elsewhere. It was home.

Fifteen minutes later, I opened the gate to my garden and stopped for a few moments, as I always did, to admire my home in the dusk, pride welling up in my heart.

I'd fallen in love at first sight with the adorable cottage. It was built of gray stone, with blue shutters, and it was a few hundred yards from the beach. Locals called it *the principal's house.* For a long time, it had belonged to the elementary school close by, and housed the principal. When the school was closed in favor of a newer, safer one, the house had been sold, but the name had remained.

I hadn't planned on buying a house when I'd moved to Karouac. But I'd fallen so deeply in love with the cottage that I couldn't imagine someone else owning it. So I'd gone to the bank and managed to convince the officials of my ability to cover the mortgage. A few weeks later, Cécile handed me the keys, and I moved in.

I still congratulated myself on the decision every day. I loved the cottage, and I really think it loved me too.

On my way in, I absentmindedly picked up the mail. There were a few envelopes, advertisements, nothing out of the ordinary. I left them on the table next to my computer and headed into the kitchen to brew some tea. I was half asleep, but I still wanted to write a few paragraphs, just to finish the current chapter.

Holding a steaming cup of tea, I switched on my computer. While it hummed and came alive, I scanned the mail. Bill, bill, bill. Advertisement. I was about to set everything down when I caught sight of a yellowed envelope addressed to an Amélie Lacombe. There was a post office label stuck to it:

We apologize for the late delivery.

That was it. No other explanation.

I frowned. Amélie Lacombe . . . As far as I knew, the house had been empty for years before I bought it. I couldn't remember the name of the previous occupants, but I didn't think it was Lacombe.

Intrigued, I looked at the date on the stamp: 1971.

The letter had been sent in 1971. Over forty-five years later, it had finally reached its destination, decades after the addressee had moved out. Talk about late delivery . . .

I suddenly remembered an article I'd read a few months earlier, about a postcard that had arrived fifteen years after being mailed. It had traveled across the country, following the addressee, who had moved away. I found the story funny, and thought it would make a good novel.

And here I was, in the same situation.

I didn't need anything more to spark my imagination. I flipped the envelope over, looking for the name of the sender, but the back was blank. Damn.

I looked at the front again, examining the careful handwriting. Should I open it? Maybe I could find a clue about the person who'd written it . . . My conscience pricked at me. It was private.

And over forty-five years old.

Did privacy have an expiration date?

I debated internally for a few more seconds before I made a decision. I would open the letter, and if the content was worth it, I would do my best to send it along to the person it was meant for.

It was easier than I thought to open the envelope without damaging it. The glue had dried over time, and with a little nudge and a paper knife, the flap gave way. I delicately extracted a single sheet of paper and unfolded it. The name of an inn from La Rochelle figured in the top right corner. L'Auberge du Voyageur. Given the name of the street it was located on, rue du Port, no doubt it was an inn where people stopped before leaving by sea. I wondered if the author of the letter took a boat to somewhere. I scanned the rest of the letter. A few paragraphs sprawled in the center of the page, the handwriting bold and assertive.

La Rochelle, September 21, 1971

My darling, my love,
It has been three weeks now since I last saw you. Three weeks during which only the memory of your perfume, of your voice whispering loving words in my ear, of the softness of your skin beneath my hands, of the taste of your kisses, have stopped me from going mad. Every hour, every second away

from you is a torment. I miss you, my Amélie, my angel, my sweetheart. I miss you more than I can express, more than anything. I cannot, will not live without you.

Please come join me, Lili. Join me and marry me. I will leave the Compagnons and follow you wherever you go, to the end of the world if need be. I know enough now to do anything, anywhere. As long as you are with me, it doesn't matter where I am or what I do . . . I need only you. Nothing else matters.

Please, Lili, write to me, come and find me at the address above. The owner is a friend, she'll let me know. I will wait for you there, or for a word from you, every evening, as long as I can, for two, three weeks, a month if I have to. Write to me, I beg you, tell me you will come . . .

I love you.

E.

I don't know how many times I reread the letter. Five, six, ten? After ten minutes, I could recite every word from memory.

I had never read anything like it. I could feel the desperation, the love the sender had for Amélie. With a pang, I suddenly realized she had never received the letter.

She had never known E was waiting for her.

A million questions whirled through my mind.

Had the sender waited for her for days, weeks, months, as promised, only to be disappointed each day? Had he written another letter? Had Amélie known that her lover waited for her in La Rochelle? What had happened next? Had he gone on without her, or had he gone back to find her?

The mysterious letter captured both my professional curiosity as a historian and my imagination as a writer. Several theories and scenarios were already taking form in my mind. Had they found each other again? Or had fate and the whim of the post office kept them apart ever since?

Slowly, with great care, I folded the letter again, slipped it into the envelope, and put it away in a drawer. Then I switched off my computer without even opening my document file.

I knew there was no point trying to write tonight. My mind was elsewhere.

With Lili and the mysterious E.

Karouac, Brittany
July 14, 1971

The party was going strong.

It was *le quatorze juillet*, a day of celebration, the anniversary of the Storming of the Bastille, which started the French Revolution some 182 years before. Nowadays, cities and towns were still celebrating the event, each in their own way. In Paris, there was a huge parade, broadcast on TV, where the army marched down the avenue des Champs-Elysées; but most towns, like Karouac, celebrated with an open-air dance, and later, around midnight, fireworks.

Sitting at the bar, Erwan was chatting with a few friends as he absentmindedly watched people cut across the dance floor, or what passed for one, to the sound of the drums and guitar played by a local rock band. A stage had been set up for the young musicians, and a few chairs and tables were available, where the dancers could rest between numbers.

Erwan sipped at his drink. He had to admit the cider wasn't very good, nor was the band, really, but he didn't care. The atmosphere of the party was carefree and fun, and that was exactly what he was looking for.

A few weeks from now, his contract in Karouac would end, and he would pack his bags and move on to the next mission. He couldn't wait. He wanted to see new places, discover new things, travel as far as he could. It felt as if he'd learned everything he could here, and now he longed for new challenges, and new people.

He'd arrived in Karouac nearly a year ago, as a brand-new aspiring Compagnon, to hone his skills as a stonemason with the Compagnons du Devoir. It was his first assignment, and he was exhilarated. The residents had welcomed him with hospitality and warmth, just like any other stranger passing through. And he had soon realized that he would never be anything more than that. He could tell from the look in their eyes, their handshakes, their politeness. He was, and always would remain, a stranger. Which, in the end, was just as well, really—it would be easier to leave when the time came.

Movement on his left caught his eye, and . . . he saw her. She was with another girl her age—seventeen-ish—and a younger one. All three stood back from the dance floor, watching the dancers. Her A-line dress was red, sleeveless, with a large white belt that sat low on her hips, and she wore a white headband in her red hair. Erwan swallowed, and his heart beat faster in his chest. She was gorgeous.

Her friend said something and she laughed. From where he was, Erwan could not hear her, but he could see every expression on her face, and he was utterly fascinated.

The girl's gaze swept over the crowd and caught his. She stared at him for a few moments, and he grew bold enough to smile at her. She smiled back, and it was as though fireworks had started just above his head. She nodded, still holding his gaze.

They maintained eye contact until a young man came up to her and asked her to dance. Casting a last glance at Erwan, the girl accepted and moved onto the dance floor.

"I'll get us drinks," France said when they sat down, later on. "Come on, Chantale, you can help carry the drinks."

"I'd rather stay with Amélie!"

"How am I going to carry all the glasses, then? It's her birthday, we can't make her work. Up you get!"

"Fine, I'm coming."

Amused, Amélie watched the teenager drag her feet as she followed her older sister. Her best friend liked to remind her baby sister who was the boss, as compensation for the fact that their parents made her take Chantale with her everywhere.

She watched as they moved toward the bar, then she scanned the dance floor, searching for one particular face she could not find. She heaved an inward sigh. She'd hoped the young man who'd caught her eye earlier would ask her to dance. Her heart beat slightly faster as she remembered the way he'd looked at her—he'd been too far away for her to be able to distinguish the color of his eyes—the way he'd smiled, how his brown, slightly unruly hair had seemed to refuse to lie completely flat. He'd been sitting, so she hadn't been able to tell for sure, but she thought he was tall and broad-shouldered. Barely older than she was—eighteen, as of today. One more step toward her majority, and the ability to make her own decisions without her parents' approval. The upcoming discussion filled her with apprehension—she would need their signature and God knew conversation with them has never been easy . . .

"Would you like to dance?"

The voice behind her jolted her out of her thoughts and the dangerous path they'd taken, and she jumped. One hand over her heart, she turned around and found herself facing the man she'd been thinking about a few seconds earlier.

His gray eyes met hers.

She barely took the time to think before answering. "Yes."

Throwing an apologetic glance at France, who was coming back with the drinks, Chantale in tow, Amélie took his hand and followed him onto the dance floor. His hands were strong and calloused, workers' hands. She wondered what he did for a living. She'd never seen him before, but that didn't necessarily mean anything. She boarded at a totally boring private school a few dozen kilometers away, and only came home to Karouac during the holidays. Fortunately, she could count on her best friend for company; she and France always had fun.

They stepped onto the dance floor, and the young man turned toward her. He smiled and wordlessly led her into a series of dance steps to the rhythm of the music, his gaze fixed on hers.

When the music stopped, he did not release her; neither did he move away, thank her, or escort her back to her friends. Instead, he looked at her.

"Would you—"

"Yes," she said, her breath short.

They danced again. And again. And again. After a couple of lively songs, the band launched into a slower piece. The young man did not ask, but laid a hand on her waist, shy and bold at the same time, seized her right hand with his left, and pulled her toward him. Amélie did not resist.

It was exactly what she wanted—for him to hold her.

"Erwan," he whispered into her ear after a few seconds' silence. "My name is Erwan."

"I'm Amélie."

"A pleasure, Amélie." He bowed his head ever so slightly.

She smiled and did the same. "Likewise."

Chapter 2

The following Saturday, I decided to visit my father's antiques shop in Lannion. I hadn't been able to stop thinking about the letter. I needed to tell someone about it, and my father was the obvious choice. For as long as I could remember, he had been my number-one confidant. He'd always been the person I turned to when I wanted advice or felt the need to talk with someone. He and the members of the knitting circle were my closest friends.

By midafternoon, I had finished marking essays—my own version of a never-ending hell—and drove into Lannion.

The delightfully old-fashioned little bell that hung over the door rang when I entered the shop, some fifteen minutes later, and I immediately felt as though I had stepped back in time. I was a little girl once again, it was Saturday afternoon, and I was rummaging through the many odds and ends in my father's little shop.

I slowly walked up the aisles I had known all my life. In the back of the shop, my father called out, "I'll be with you right away!"

"One day, someone will walk out with all your stuff if you keep leaving it unattended like this," I told him when he emerged from the back a few moments later. I kissed him on the cheek.

"My favorite daughter!"

"Papa, I'm your only daughter."

"Which does not preclude your being my favorite, Flavie. How are you?"

"Good. You?"

"Better than good. I've just received a truly stunning piece of work! Here, have a look."

He stepped around the counter to fetch his "stunning piece of work." It was indeed beautiful—a weathered mahogany jewelry box, probably from the late nineteenth century, with several drawers, including a hidden one my father eagerly pulled out for me to see.

"I found the drawer while I was cleaning it."

"Is there anything inside?" I asked, curious.

"Unfortunately, no."

"What do you think it could have held? Love letters? A shopping list?"

"A winning lottery ticket, tucked away by the owner, who didn't want anybody to know about her gambling, until she forgot all about it?"

"And nobody ever claimed the money . . ."

"What a great story!"

It was a game we used to play when I was a little girl. On Saturday afternoons, I would do my homework in the back of his shop, sitting in my father's massive, velvet-covered armchair. I felt like a grown-up with my books spread over his dark oak desk. I would hurry through my homework, eager to join my father in the next room and make up stories with him.

Papa always checked my homework. He would go over my math, and listen to me stuttering my times tables. And once we were done, he would choose an object from his shop, and for the next few hours, we would amuse ourselves by inventing outlandish, extravagant, romantic, or melodramatic stories about it. The one who came up with the best story would get to choose what we'd have for dinner. Funnily enough, it was usually me . . . at the time, I really thought I was very creative.

These days, when I think about all the hours we spent wondering about some object's past, tracing the path of a famous historical figure's adventures on an old map of the world, I credit my father for inspiring me to be a writer. Stories had opened up my mind to a world of imagination, and my father's tales had been just as much, if not more, of a factor than our bedtime stories. I loved listening to his voice unraveling the chapters of history, of great men and strangers alike. From time to time, I still ask him to tell me a story, purely for the sake of feeling as though I am ten years old again.

I smiled as the memories rushed into my mind. "I love it when we do that," I said.

"Yes, like in the good old days," Papa said with a glint of nostalgia in his eyes.

"Indeed."

He set the jewelry box down and met my gaze. "Now, what's the matter, sweetheart?"

"Do I need a reason to visit my father and his marvelous shop?"

"Of course not." There was something both paternal and infinitely sweet in his face. "But Flavie, my dear, you forget I know you better than anyone else. And there's something behind today's visit."

I'd never been able to hide anything from him. "You're right. There is something I'd like to show you."

I'd slipped the letter in a plastic baggie to protect it before tucking it into my purse. I unfolded it and handed it to my father, who adjusted his glasses and examined the letter carefully. After reading it, he looked at me, his gaze speculative.

I knew that look. I'd been wearing the same one ever since I'd opened the envelope.

"What are you going to do?"

I hesitated. "What do you think I should do?"

"If I were you . . . I think I'd try to find out more. Just to appease my nagging curiosity."

I smiled, unsurprised. The apple never falls far from the tree. "You'll be happy to hear that's exactly what I've decided to do."

He smiled back at me. "I never doubted it. You probably already have a battle plan all thought out."

"You really do know me too well."

"I've been your father for the last twenty-nine years. I have some practice!"

"That does help," I conceded.

"Tell me everything."

I did exactly that. I told him about all the plans I'd made, all the stories I'd imagined.

I was ten years old again, and we were making up extravagant and elaborate tales. Except this time, I fully intended to put my ideas into action. My inner historian had awoken from her slumber and was ready and raring to go on an adventure to explore the past.

I was determined to unravel this mystery.

* * *

I wasted no time in executing the plan my father and I had drawn up. On Monday morning, as soon as I had a break between classes, I called the elementary school to set up a meeting with the principal.

I had very little information on the person who had sent the letter—a mere initial at the bottom of the page, and the fact that he had been a Compagnon at the time. I had therefore decided to start my investigation with Amélie and the principal's house. There ought to be at least one person who could help me find out who had lived there in the past, and that was surely the current principal. And even if they didn't know, they would have access to the school archives, if there were any.

In any case, I had to start somewhere, and the school seemed the safest bet.

Unfortunately, the only meeting time available was Tuesday evening. I would have to skip knit night . . . but I needed this interview, so I accepted anyway, and texted everyone an apology, promising to tell them everything as soon as possible.

The principal of Karouac's elementary school was an athletic, fairly attractive man in his midthirties, with a charming smile. If he'd taught middle school, like I did, he would have been very popular with the ladies of all ages.

"How can I help you, Ms. Richalet?" he asked after we shook hands and I had politely declined his offer of coffee.

"Please call me Flavie. I'm only Ms. Richalet to my students."

"Are you a teacher, then?"

"I am, but my students are a bit older than yours. I teach history and geography at the Lannion middle school."

"How can I help, then, Flavie?"

I'd thought long and hard about this. How much should I tell people in order to explain my questions? Should I mention the letter and its contents, or go with something vaguer? What if they didn't understand my curiosity? What if they thought I was foolish? In the end, I'd decided to tread the middle path.

"I recently found an old letter dating back to 1971 mentioning a name, as well as the old principal's house, and I grew curious about it. I decided to investigate a little, see if I could find out anything more. You know us historians—we only need the slightest pretext to start rummaging around archives to try to unearth old stories."

Then I added, "I know that the house used to be part of the school, and I was hoping there would be some archives around here that I could have a look at, maybe a place to start."

"I see. I don't think I'm going to be much help, unfortunately. There was a flood a few years back and all of the archives from earlier than 1986 were lost." He seemed regretful. "I'm sorry. I wish I could help you."

Drat! I was off to a bad start. I had really hoped to find something here. *Okay, this isn't the end of it. I still have a few leads to follow. There should be someone, somewhere, who lived in Karouac in the seventies who can help me. I just need to . . . find that person.*

I stood up. "Well, thanks anyway. I'll rethink my approach and have a look somewhere else. I'm sorry I wasted your time," I added with a slight grimace.

"Don't worry about it. I wish I could have been more help."

"Before I leave, maybe you know someone who could help me?"

"Let me think about it . . . I don't believe so . . . Wait a minute! There's Chantale Dumas. I bet she could help."

"Chantale?"

"She's one of our teachers. She's been a part of our staff for a long time, I actually think she's spent her entire career here. Why don't you give me your number, and I'll ask her tomorrow if she'd be willing to speak to you."

My disappointment vanished instantly, just as my hopes soared. "I would love to meet her, if she'd agree." I tried to keep my voice as steady as possible. "Thank you so much, sir. I'm very grateful for your help."

"Please call me Christophe. I'm only *sir* to my students."

"Very well." I was amused at the nod to our earlier exchange. "Christophe."

"I'll speak with Ms. Dumas and get back to you."

"Thank you, Christophe. I'll be waiting to hear from you."

I nearly skipped on my way home. I couldn't stop smiling. If Ms. Dumas had taught here all her life, there was a good chance she knew a lot of things about the town. Maybe she'd even known the principal in the seventies!

Over the last week, I'd done a fair amount of thinking about the mysterious Amélie's identity. My mystery man called her "Lili." A quick Google search hadn't yielded anything yet, though with essays to mark and lessons to prepare, I hadn't been able to give it much time. In any case, I had so few clues that finding anything from a time before the internet was like searching for a needle in a haystack. I didn't even know if Amélie had lived in my house, or if she'd been there as a visitor. Was she perhaps related to the principal? I needed to know more about her if I wanted to figure out the mystery of the lost letter.

While I was waiting for news from Christophe, I took advantage of the fact there was no school on Wednesday afternoon, as is customary in primary and secondary schools, to visit the town hall and search for clues, meager though they might be.

The secretary at the desk behind the counter smiled politely as I came in.

"Good afternoon. How may I help you?"

"Hi. I'm looking for information on the people who lived in the principal's house in the seventies. In 1971, to be precise."

"May I ask why?"

I told her the same thing I'd told Christophe, about finding a letter and trying to find out more.

She frowned. "All right. But what do you need from me?"

"Well, the house used to belong to the town. I thought maybe you would have a list of the former tenants. Maybe you could tell me who used to live there, or the name of the principal at the time. That would be really helpful."

She hesitated. "We probably have the information somewhere, but I'm not sure if I can give it to you without some sort of legal authorization. You'd have to go to the town archives and ask someone there for help."

"Oh, sorry! I thought maybe you could help me."

"Sorry, miss, but that's not really part of my job. I'm pretty sure the only place someone could assist you in your search is at the archives. At the very least, they can probably answer your questions."

Well, that was another dead end. I'd suspected it wasn't the kind of information they just handed out to anyone, but I'd been willing to take a chance. I certainly wasn't going to neglect any leads, so the archives would be my next stop.

As soon as my various professional obligations would allow me to, anyway—essays to grade, teachers' conferences to prepare for, field trips to organize . . . The usual stuff that popped up around this time of the year.

"Thanks, I will. Could you repeat the address for me?"

Karouac, Brittany
July 14, 1971

"You should get back to your friends, they might be worried," Erwan whispered, more out of a sense of duty than any kind of inclination. He didn't want the evening to end. Nor did he want to leave. Not yet.

The fireworks had long since fizzled out, and the crowd had slowly left the beach, until they were the only two left. The only sounds now were the low rush of waves and the faint notes of music from the party, still in full swing.

They'd danced together all evening, never separating, gazing into each other's eyes. When the fireworks had raced up into the sky, their hands had brushed, almost as if by accident. Even as their gazes had been fixed on the colorful lights in the night sky, the touch of her hand had thrilled him, and unaccustomed emotions welled up inside him. He felt as though he could soar. King of the world!

He most certainly did not want their evening to end. He wished it could go on forever, that tomorrow would never come, that all their obligations could vanish as though by magic, that the only possible future was on this beach, by her side. He wanted to drown in her eyes and never come up for air.

He looked down into her eyes, shyly, waiting for her answer with bated breath.

"No," she said quietly, as though she had guessed what was on his mind. "Not yet. I . . . I don't want to go back yet. It's nice here, isn't it?"

Relieved, Erwan smiled, then stood up and extended a hand to her.

"In that case, my lady, would you honor me with another dance?"

Chapter 3

"Okay, spill. Why'd you skip the knitting circle on Tuesday? And you better have a solid excuse. I'm talking I-met-Prince-Charming type of excuse."

I swallowed a mouthful of cupcake before I answered. After I missed our meeting, my friends' curiosity had rocketed straight up to somewhere around the level of their weekly sugar intake. Hence the reason we were having an impromptu Thursday meeting, after school/visiting/closing hours, so I could tell them all the juicy details. We had gathered in the kitchen of Bérénice's shop, greedily swallowing the day's leftover pastries.

"Trust me, it's close enough!"

"You met someone?" The cry rang out from all directions at once. "Tell us everything!"

"I didn't meet someone, exactly. Not face-to-face, in any case."

I wiped my hand carefully before I extracted the letter from my purse and read it out loud. For the next few moments, the only sound to be heard was Olivier, Angélique's baby, gurgling happily.

"How'd you come across it?" Bérénice finally asked.

"It was in my mail when I came home on Tuesday, last week. Apparently it was lost somewhere in a post office drawer and its delivery was 'slightly delayed,'" I said, jabbing air quotes with my fingers.

"Forty-five years is one hell of a delay, if you ask me," Vic retorted.

"Better late than never," I said.

"Except in this case it has not reached its intended recipient."

"What are you going to do with it?" Bérénice asked.

"I don't know yet. I've started digging a little, to try to see if I can find something out about either of these people."

"Have you?"

"Not yet, but I do have a few leads."

I summarized my conversation with the elementary school's principal and outlined my plan to visit the town archives if the school teacher could not or would not help me.

"I'll decide on the next step then. If I can figure out E's full name, I could make some inquiries with the Compagnons du Devoir. He seems to have been one. The clerk at the city hall couldn't give me details about that either. She barely knew what I was talking about, so I don't have enough information yet, but maybe later..."

"Please refresh my memory, Flavie. The Compagnons... That's the guild-like organization that dates back to the Middle Ages and trains craftsmen by having them travel all over France to work in different places?"

"That's the one."

"That's still a thing?"

"It is! And to my great surprise, it's actually thriving."

"Well, that's always one lead you can come back to. You don't have a lot of information, which makes asking the Compagnons a bit premature for now." Cécile was ever the pragmatic one. "You need to find out more about him."

"Exactly." I nodded.

"What do you think happened between Amélie and E?" Bérénice wondered. "Do you think they found each other again?"

"I don't think so." Vic's tone was unequivocal. "He probably kept waiting, and waiting, hoping she'd come back."

"'Baby come back,'" Cécile sang under her breath, teasing.

"Or," Bérénice went on, her imagination stirring, "he was madly in love and he went back to get her. They eloped together and they now live in a sunny little southern town. And that's where we'll find them."

"I think it was a long and tortuous tale," I chimed in, amused by our what-if game. "They found and lost each other several times, they ended up married to different people, but both marriages were unhappy, and ten years later they had a quiet wedding in a little church. The only people present were their best friends serving as best man and maid of honor. They had triplets who brought about their own little happily-ever-after..."

"Hey, I have an idea!" Cécile interjected. "We should bet on it!"

"Bet?" Flavie asked.

"Yeah! Whoever gets closest to what really happened wins."

"Why would we do that?"

"Why not? It'd be fun! We each write our theories on a piece of paper, sign it and put it in a box, and once Flavie has ferreted out the truth—and knowing her, I have no doubt that she will—we open the box and find out who was closest. Whoever is furthest from the truth gets a penalty." Cécile was on a roll.

"What about the winner?" Angélique wondered.

"I don't know . . . She can choose something!" said Vic enthusiastically.

"We need an impartial observer," Angélique said, starting to plan out the game.

"My father could referee," Flavie offered.

"Good idea!" Angélique agreed.

"You willing?" Cécile asked, when Bérénice remained silent.

"I don't know . . ." Bérénice said.

"Well, count me in!" Vic chimed in.

"Come on, Bérénice, it'll be fun!" Cécile said, trying to win her over.

"Okay, okay, I'm in."

"Yessss!"

Snugly settled in his baby seat, Olivier watched us with round eyes, probably wondering who these crazy people were, getting so excited over a dumb game.

We clinked our cupcakes together as though they were champagne glasses to seal the deal, and Olivier's giggling provided our very own soundtrack.

The principal, Christophe, called me back on Saturday morning. I was elbow-deep in marking my students' tests.

He didn't waste any time telling me that Chantale Dumas was willing to meet and would wait for me in her classroom after school next Monday, if that suited me. It did, and I accepted at once. Come Monday afternoon, I rushed my last class just a tiny bit so I could join her as quickly as possible. I was impatient to learn anything Chantale knew about Amélie.

Chantale Dumas was somewhere between fifty and sixty, and silver-haired. She had warm blue eyes and a mellow voice that was slightly hoarse. Her face, her smile, the kindness I could see in her gaze set me at ease immediately. I would have loved to have learned math from her instead of the old shrew that had been my own teacher when I was in primary school. Maybe I'd have been good at numbers instead of barely hanging on.

"Please, have a seat," she said softly when I entered the classroom.

"Thank you for meeting me, Ms. Dumas. I'm very grateful." I sat opposite her in one of the children's chairs. "Your classroom is wonderful," I added as I looked around.

Like most classrooms, a huge map of the world was pinned on one of the walls. I smiled as I remembered that my own classroom held the same one. At the very top of the walls, just under the ceiling, a hand-drawn frieze related major historical events. It looked as though the children had drawn it themselves. Everything on the teacher's desk was neatly organized, and the green chalkboard still bore traces of the last lesson. Conjugating verbs, apparently.

It smelled like happy childhood.

"Thank you."

"This brings back so many memories," I murmured.

She frowned. "I don't think I remember you. Were you in my class?"

"No, I grew up with my father in Lannion, and I went to school there. But there's a certain atmosphere in classrooms that you find in every school, don't you agree?"

"I most certainly do. Tell me, Ms. Richalet, how can I help you?"

"Please call me Flavie. Did the principal tell you what I am looking for?"

"He just said you were researching something and wanted to talk to someone who lived in Karouac in the seventies."

"That's about the size of it."

"Well, you came to the right place. I was born in Karouac and I've lived here all my life. So what do you want to know?"

I could hardly believe my ears. All her life? Six decades in Karouac? This was even better than I'd dared to hope.

"Actually, I'm looking for information on the people who used to live in the former principal's house."

"In the seventies?" Her brow furrowed, and she cocked her head to one side, eyes half shut, paying very close attention all of a sudden.

"Yes. As I told the principal, I found a document from 1971 mentioning a name and linking it back to the house. I was intrigued and wanted to know more."

"In 1971 . . . What was the name?"

There was a strange light in Ms. Dumas's eyes.

"Amélie, Amélie Lacombe."

I held my breath. *Please let her know the name, please let her know the name . . .*

A smile stretched across her wrinkled face. "Amélie . . . Of course . . . Who else?"

My heart leapt. "You . . . you know her?"

She nodded. "I know her quite well. She's my older sister's best friend."

Chapter 4

"Your sister's best friend?" I exclaimed.

Even in my wildest dreams, I hadn't expected to find one of Amélie's acquaintances so fast. And not just any acquaintance— her best friend's younger sister! Things were looking up. Maybe I'd learn that the lovebirds had reunited, and would discover who the mysterious E was!

Then something she said sunk in.

Something beyond the fact that she knew Amélie.

"Wait. You *know* her? Present tense? As in, you're still in touch with her?"

"I'm not, but my sister still exchanges Christmas and birthday cards with her. I hear a few things now and then, just like when I was a child."

This was getting better and better. I felt like I'd just won the lottery.

"What can you tell me about her?"

Ms. Dumas smiled, a touch of nostalgia on her face. "So much, and so little . . . She was lovely. I suppose she still is. She had the kind of beauty that time has no effect on. Unlike me."

I was about to protest, but she waved my reply away.

"No need to pretend, I know the years haven't been exactly kind to me. But Amélie was something else."

"What was she like?"

"She was tall, a redhead. She had the most beautiful green eyes. She was a lively woman, very active, constantly sketching. Her dream was to become a fashion designer, and Coco Chanel was her role model. But I know her parents disagreed. They wanted her to become a doctor. They had several arguments about it the summer before she left for university in Paris. I think it might be the year of the document you found . . . Yes, it was. I was thirteen, so it was in 1971."

"How old was she?"

"She's my sister's age and we're five years apart, so she'd have been eighteen."

Eighteen . . . So young.

"Did she win the argument? Did she become a designer?"

"She did. She was accepted in a Paris university and she begged her parents to let her go. In the end, they relented, even though they were disappointed she didn't pursue the brilliant medical career they'd envisioned for her. But she wanted to become a designer and she did. I think she even created her own clothing line with a catchy little name . . . It's on the tip of my tongue . . . Lili K! That's the one."

Lili . . . The nickname the mysterious E had given her . . .

Did that mean they were still together? I tried to keep a tight rein on my imagination before it swept me away.

Facts, Flavie. Focus on the facts. Forget about being a writer and creating stories from the smallest tidbits. Today, you're here as a historian, and a historian only.

Easier said than done.

"In any case, I'm impressed you can remember that, forty-five years later!"

"I have a very good memory. Too good, on occasion. I still remember entire conversations from when I was young, and trust me, I'd rather forget all about them."

"It's still very impressive."

"It was also the last summer we spent together, which makes it easier to remember."

"What happened after that?"

"Life happened. She and my sister moved to Paris to go to university. They stuck to each other like glue. Amélie rarely came back to Karouac. She got married and went to live in the south of France, where her husband's family lived. I didn't hear from her very often after that. Sometimes my sister would pass on some news, though it's been a long time since she last told me anything."

My heart missed a beat.

"You said she got married . . . Do you remember her husband's name?"

"Panivello. Paul Panivello. They got divorced a few years later, if I remember well. They had two children, girls I think."

Paul. Not a name that started with an E. Disappointment welled up inside me. The story was not unraveling the way I'd pictured. And none of this gave me a clue as to who E was, or what had happened to him if he hadn't been the one to marry Amélie.

His *Lili* . . .

Who was he?

"During that summer . . . in 1971," I finally ventured. "Do you know if something happened? If she . . . met someone? A boy, maybe?"

Ms. Dumas pondered this for a minute, deep in thought. "Now that you mention it . . . There was a young man. My sister and Amélie were often whispering together. They'd stop whenever I came near them, but I recall that there was a boy she danced with all evening at the Bastille Day party. I never saw him again, but I remember thinking he was quite handsome."

"Do you remember his name?"

"I don't think I ever knew. I'm not sure . . . I seem to recall Amélie saying he was part of the team restoring the old church, but she might have been talking about someone else. I was eavesdropping, so I didn't hear everything clearly," she admitted, looking sheepish.

"Eavesdropping? A fine hobby for a teacher!" I laughed.

"I wasn't a teacher at the time," she argued back, smiling. "I was thirteen and I had an older sister who was rarely pleased to have me clinging to her skirts. She never told me anything, so I had to be sneaky if I wanted to satisfy my curiosity. I often eavesdropped on her and Amélie. I couldn't help it—I was fascinated by Amélie. I wanted to be like her: beautiful, smart, and determined. All young girls need a hero, and Amélie was mine."

That was true. Mine had been my mother, until the day she'd packed up and left without looking back. My father had become my hero after that.

He still is.

"Well, in any case, thank you for speaking with me."

"I hope that was helpful. What are you going to do now? Write a novel about it?"

She was joking, but the idea immediately seized hold of me. Dug its way into my mind.

Write a novel. Tell this story. Correct the mistakes of the past through my writing.

Why didn't I think of it earlier? Now that the idea was spinning in my head, it seemed so obvious. It was the perfect outline for a story full of emotion and tearful reunions. Because in my story, they would find their way back to each other. That was nonnegotiable. Whatever had happened in real life, as long as I was the writer, my heroine would spend the rest of her days with the love of her life.

They were made for each other, of that I was utterly convinced. Why would Amélie have divorced otherwise? My mind immediately started coming up with a thousand alternatives, but I batted them aside.

In my own version, E was the man of Amélie's dreams, and they would end up together. End of story.

E and his Lili . . . In my mind, I could already see how this was going to end.

"Flavie?"

Ms. Dumas's question brought me back to reality. Once again, I'd let my imagination run away with me. "Sorry, I was already outlining the story in my head. In the beginning, I was just trying to find some answers, but you're right—it would be a great idea to write this story. I'll think about it."

Chantale smiled, and I hesitated.

"Would you, by any chance, have Amélie's address or phone number?"

"Unfortunately not, but I can ask my sister. She's in Canada right now with her husband, but I can call her when they get back."

"Thank you, I'd really appreciate that."

"It's a plan, then. I'll let you know."

She hesitated. "Can I ask you something?"

"Of course!"

"I'm a little curious . . . What kind of document did you find that mentioned Amélie?"

I only hesitated for a moment before I answered. I owed her that much—she'd practically offered up everything I wanted to know on a silver platter. And deep down, I knew I could trust her.

"It was a letter."

Chapter 5

Over the next two weeks, I spent all my free time—which was getting scarce as the end of the school year grew near—surfing the internet to try to find out more about Amélie-Lili and E and all that had happened that summer. I was determined to turn this story into a novel and I needed to know everything.

I used all the combinations of keywords I could think of, but despite my efforts, the results were meager. It had been easy to find Lili K on the internet, and her collection of vintage clothing with its modern accents and a touch of seventies style had instantly won me over.

After that, I had read all the articles I could unearth on her—and there were very few—as well as all the information that was provided on the website of the store that sold her brand. That's how I discovered that though she had worked as an independent designer for much of her life, about ten years ago she decided to sell Lili K—which was apparently the name of her brand as well as the name Amelie used professionally—to a retail chain that offered her a more important outreach. There were a few shops scattered throughout the country, but unfortunately none nearby. I jotted down the addresses anyway, made notes of everything that could be useful for my novel, and many other things that weren't.

But the one thing I couldn't find was the one thing that I needed most: her contact information. Neither the retail store website nor the online phone directory, where I searched Amelie's married and maiden names, offered me a number to call or an email address to which I could write. For one moment, I envisioned contacting the human resources department of the retail chain, but I doubted that they would divulge her contact information to a stranger. In the end, my best shot was probably waiting for Chantale to give me her address or phone number so I could reach out to her . . . And maybe find some answers. Like information concerning the K that intrigued me so much.

Much to my regret, I had no more luck in uncovering the mysterious E's identity. Based on what Chantale had told me, I'd pulled up the Karouac city website and gone through the town history tab. The only thing I'd been able to confirm had been that part of the church had burnt down in 1970 and that restoration work had lasted over a year. No Compagnons had been mentioned. I was starting to despair that I'd ever discover E's identity. Maybe I'd have to ask Amélie when I finally tracked her down. But would she be willing to tell me?

I was aware that I was digging into the private lives of people who had no connection to me, blood or otherwise. The only link between us was the letter. Hopefully they were both still alive. I knew very well that I had gone well beyond the boundaries of simple curiosity and that what I was doing could hardly be called "historical research." But I had gone too far to stop now.

I needed to know.

I needed to find them. Both of them.

After two weeks, I still hadn't heard back from Chantale. I didn't dare call her, fearing that would be too presumptuous, so I laid out all the information I had and asked my father's and my friends' advice. In the end, I decided to go through the local newspaper's archives in the hope of finding something about the restoration work, maybe even a few names, before I went to speak with the current priest in Karouac.

That was how I found myself, one Wednesday afternoon after my classes were done, entering the office of the local branch of the Breton newspaper. Disregarding the many test papers I still had to grade, I started digging through the microfilm of newspapers printed between 1970 and 1971.

In my bright-eyed enthusiasm, I launched a keyword search, confident that the files had been indexed. I soon discovered I was totally wrong. It was impossible to search through the files by keyword. Only one solution remained—go through all the microfilm for the period from May 1970, when the church had burned down, to September 1971, when the letter had been sent. Which meant skimming through 547 issues, which in turn meant 8,207 pages printed in Times New

Roman 8. At least the titles were in size 18 font—if I had to read everything, I'd be in here for the next few weeks.

I had to go over to the archives six times, spending many hours of my Wednesday and Saturday afternoons the following weeks, before I discovered the information I was looking for. Though the time I spent poring over the newspapers allowed me to uncover a hoard of interesting facts that would probably be very useful when I wrote my novel, it was also fuel for much false joy and many wasted hours.

But I instantly forgot my disappointment and my frustration at the time I'd spent boxed in the narrow room when I finally discovered something useful. It was an article reporting progress on the church repairs. I'd already found a few, as reporters tended to feel obligated to detail each step of the restoration. But this was a more general article, and it had a picture accompanying it, featuring the skilled workers to whom Karouac owed a functional, beautiful, almost as good as new church. There was a caption below the photograph listing the names of the workers, from left to right: Denis Breton, François Delaporte, Gérard Beaulieu and Benoît Arnoux, all qualified builders and stonemasons, and young aspiring Compagnon Erwan Kermarrec. All five worked under the supervision of Daniel Bourgeois, the general contractor and head of the masonry company hired by the town, top right on the photograph, himself a Compagnon.

I stilled.

Erwan Kermarrec, aspiring Compagnon. It fit perfectly. The initial E, the near-Compagnon status . . . I had found Amélie's mysterious lover. It had to be him.

Erwan Kermarrec.

With a K. Was it the same K as in *Lili K*? If it was, why had Amélie added Erwan Kermarrec's initial to her creation if she'd married another man? Questions and conjectures whirled through my mind, and I was dangerously close to throwing caution to the winds and pressing Chantale to give me Amélie's address, manners be damned.

Instead, I printed the article and studied the picture. It was small and grainy, but I thought Chantale had been right. Erwan was handsome. Early twenties, square jaw, charming smile . . . And unruly hair. If he hadn't looked a little shy, he would have been the perfect bad boy.

I smiled. I could understand why Amélie had fallen in love with him. He was terribly cute, in his own way.

I slipped the article into my notebook and continued to look, galvanized by my success, hoping there would be other articles about Erwan.

There was just one, dated September 1, 1971, entitled "A New Virgin Mary for the Karouac Church." The reporter, one Solenn Perrec, explained that the Karouac parish had received a foot-and-a-half-tall stone Virgin Mary as a gift from a promising young sculptor, Erwan Kermarrec. After a year working under the direction of Daniel Bourgeois during his Tour de France, she went on, young Erwan had offered the church an art piece he had sculpted during the time he'd spent in Karouac. She concluded by informing readers that Erwan had left the town that same morning to head out to his next post, and wishing him luck. A picture of Erwan's statue accompanied the article. Unfortunately, it was in black and white and very little could be seen.

At the end of the day, I had found nothing more to help me recreate Amélie and Erwan's story. I leaned back in my chair, gazing at the two articles I'd unearthed and printed, wondering if the statue was still there—and in that case, if I could have a look at it.

The next day, after school, I decided to go and see the statue Erwan had sculpted. Now that I knew his name, I had stopped using his initial. Holding the article I'd printed, I stepped through the door, crossed myself—a remnant of a Catholic education I cannot seem to let go, despite my best efforts—and stopped in my tracks, dazzled by the beauty around me.

It may seem strange, but though I'd been living in Karouac for five years, I had never set foot in the church. Not even to visit it, which was unusual enough for someone who calls herself a historian and should, by definition, live in the past. I'd visited all the surrounding castles, as well as all the historical monuments, but I'd never come here. Better late than never, my father always says, and I was finally mending my ways.

The church was magnificent. Romanesque architecture, probably dating back to the sixteenth or seventeenth century, it was simple and modest, but wide, bright, and comfortable. Tall stone pillars separated the central nave from lower side-aisles. Light streamed through an incredible array of colored glass, and the inside of the church positively glowed.

I hugged the leather satchel, which held both articles as well as all my notes, to my chest. I slowly walked between the pews, feeling as though I needed more eyes to take everything in. I reached the transept and looked around for Erwan's Virgin Mary. Finding nothing, I went over to the priest who had just entered.

"Hello, Father. Can I ask you something?"

"Of course. How can I help you? I am Father François," he added with a smile.

I opened my leather satchel and showed him the article. "I'm looking for this statue."

"Ah, young Erwan's Virgin Mary. Follow me."

The priest led me to a hidden corner on the left end of the transept and pointed. "Here it is."

I drew closer to examine it. It was indeed the statue from the photograph. I lingered over the face, a pure, exquisite shape, though different from the usual representations. Instead of the round cheeks of an angel, Erwan's Virgin Mary had high, defined cheekbones and large, half-lidded eyes. There was a barely there smile on its lips, and its downturned face expressed quiet happiness, almost bliss.

"It's beautiful."

Out of the corner of my eye, I saw the priest nod. "It is. The sculptor was a very talented young man."

I turned to him. "Did you know him?"

"I did, and rather well, I think."

"Oh, Father, would you tell me about him? What you know of him?"

"Can I ask you why?"

I looked down, then raised my gaze to meet his. "It's a long and slightly crazy story, Father . . . In short, I happened upon a letter bearing his initial and the name of another person, a woman. I managed to trace the letter back to him, and—"

"And you'd like to know more about him?"

I nodded. "I'd like to try to find him."

"I see."

"Can you help me?"

"It was such a long time ago . . ."

"Forty-five years."

"Forty-five years . . . I was a young priest then. I still remember the day he came with this gift. He was . . . unsettled. Sad."

"How so?"

He looked embarrassed, as though he'd already said too much. "It's not my place to tell."

I felt my shoulders slump along with my hopes. My smile dropped off my face. "Of course not." I tried to hide my disappointment. "Do you know where he is now?"

"No. I haven't heard from him since he left Karouac."

"Oh, no."

"Have you tried asking the Brittany Compagnons office?"

"Not yet. That's my next step."

"They might be able to help you. I think he told me he wanted to go back to his birthplace once he'd finished his training."

"Where would that be?"

"In the Finistère"

His answer brought back memories of trips I had taken there with my father. The Finistère is the region at the very tip of Brittany, where it extends into the Atlantic Ocean, just east of Lannion and Karouac. It was incredibly beautiful there, raw and almost untouched by the human hand. There, you could find all the landscapes of Brittany gather into one place: agricultural fields and forests bordering rocky cliffs that dropped down to the stormy sea—and many typical Breton villages, wearing proudly their Celtic origins and influences.

I always thought that it was the most Breton area in all of Brittany.

Needless to say, I loved it there.

"Thank you very much," I said to Father François. "At least now I have a place to start looking."

"I'm sorry I can't be more helpful. That's all I can tell you. The rest . . . is under the seal of confession."

"I understand, Father. Thank you for your help. Have a nice day."

I was already walking away when he called me back.

"Miss?"

"Yes?" I turned back to him.

"If you do find him . . . Please ask him to let me know how he's doing, if you don't mind."

"Of course, Father, I will."

As I walked away, I wondered why Erwan had been unsettled on the day he'd given Father François the statue of the Virgin Mary.

Karouac, Brittany
August 1, 1971

Erwan pushed the heavy church door open and sat on one of the pews, setting his precious burden down beside him. He breathed in the scent of the church, that mixture of incense and the polish used on the wooden pews. This would probably be the last time he'd visit here, this place where he had spent so much time. From the very first days, he had loved the silence, the peace and serenity he had found here. He wasn't a true believer, and barely a churchgoer, but he had been raised in the Catholic faith, and some of that had stayed with him. In his eyes, a church was a place of contemplation, the perfect place to gather his thoughts.

Father François silently came up and sat next to him, as he had so often done in the past year, and waited for Erwan to speak.

"It's my last day, Father."

"You don't look happy about that. Weren't you looking forward to exploring new horizons?"

"I was. I am."

"What changed?"

"Nothing. Everything. I met the woman of my dreams. The love of my life."

"You sound very sure for someone who is still quite young."

"I'm sorry, Father, but my feelings have nothing to do with my age."

"How can you know?"

Erwan kept silent for a few moments. "How old were you when you decided to become a priest, Father?"

"Around your age, I think."

"And how did you know that was the right decision? That it was what you were meant to do?"

"I just knew."

"And I know Amélie is the love of my life."

"That's not the same thing."

"With all due respect, Father," Erwan said, "it's exactly the same thing."

Father François thought about it for a moment. "You're right, it is. What are you going to do?"

"I don't know. I don't want to lose her."

"If she's meant to be with you, you won't lose her. The Lord will reunite you, whatever may happen."

Erwan let out a skeptical laugh. "Maybe. But I'd rather rely on myself."

Father François sighed. "Ah, faithlessness . . . The plague of the younger generation!"

Erwan smiled grimly. "I came to say goodbye, Father. And leave you a gift."

"A gift?"

Wordlessly, Erwan handed over his burden.

"You shouldn't have."

"It's not much."

The priest unwrapped the cloth, revealing a statue of the Virgin Mary carved out of stone.

"Did you do this?"

Erwan nodded. "I took an old stone block that had fallen off the church that we had no use for, and I carved this for you. To thank you for all you have done."

"I didn't do anything, my son."

"You did. You were there for me. You listened to me, even when I said things you disagreed with. You never stopped me from expressing myself. And that is important to me."

"It's a beautiful gift, Erwan. I'll make sure it's treated the way it deserves. And one day, when you come back, I'll show you that I took good care of it."

Chapter 6

In addition to delving into the newspaper archives, I had also spent considerable time browsing the internet, looking up any website or Wikipedia page I could find on the Compagnons du Devoir.

I already knew a few things about the *compagnonnage*, as was called the fact of being a Compagnon. I remembered, for example, that it was a specific way of training young people—young *male* people, although in the last decades, the institution seemed to have opened itself to the twenty-first century and started to accept female students—in a specific trade, such as stonemasonry, baking, carpentry, painting, or even landscape architecture, to name but a few. It originated as a guild in the Middle Ages. But as I dug deeper into the secrets and mysteries of the centuries-old institution of the Compagnons du Devoir, I discovered that it was more, much more, than a vocational institution that offered professional training. By experiencing life in community and traveling all around the country—and sometimes even abroad—the aspiring Compagnons not only learned their trade directly on worksites, under the supervision of master craftsmen, but developed precious values like cooperation, generosity, and a thirst for knowledge, all the while developing their character and personality.

The website of the Compagnons du Devoir made me realize that the journey to become a certified and acknowledged Compagnon, which is called a Tour de France—literally a journey around France—is a very long one, and requires patience and will. It starts after the student obtains a basic diploma in the trade he or she wants to specialize in, and lasts a few years—at least six to eight. During the first year of the Tour, the student is called a *stagiaire* (Compagnon guest) and has to live in the Compagnon house, where he takes lessons and shares his life with other Compagnons. It's a kind of initiation into the Compagnon way of life. At the end of the year, the *stagiaire* may ask to officially become a member of the institution. This requires what is called a *travail d'adoption*, that is to say some kind of work demonstrating the candidate's proficiency. If the work is accepted, he becomes an aspiring Compagnon, an *aspirant*. That's when he starts working full-time, though he is still required to live in the community's house and take lessons in the evening. He begins traveling to multiple cities or towns, working on a new job at each stop in his journey. At the end of the Tour de France, after three to five years learning his trade, he presents his *travail d'réception*, the masterpiece that determines whether he becomes a fully acknowledged Compagnon.

After that, one would think that the student has earned his Compagnon title . . . but not yet! Once his masterpiece has been accepted, the student becomes a Compagnon *itinérant* (traveling Compagnon) and must tour for three more years, before he is finally allowed to live and work where he wants—provided that he volunteers to train and teach aspiring Compagnons in the house nearest to him.

Well, that's certainly a long journey, one that requires . . . well . . . motivation.

Discovering all those details helped me understand what kind of man Erwan could have become, what his values were, and most of all . . . where I could find him. Surely, the house where Erwan volunteered would have his contact information—if he was still a Compagnon, obviously, which I was rather hoping he was. If not, maybe they could direct me to a place where they kept details about former Compagnons, where I might find details about the places he went to learn his trade, some of the cities where he lived during his Tour, or something, anything, that would help me find him.

That was all I had to go on for now. Sometime during my research into the *compagnonnage*, I had called the inn where Erwan had said he would wait for Amélie, but to no avail. They hadn't been able to help me—at all. They didn't even recognize the name, the owners and staff having changed a few times during the four decades that had passed since Erwan wrote his letter. I tried the internet, but my research didn't yield results that were specific enough for my taste. I couldn't seem to find him, no matter how I looked for him.

The Compagnon houses were thus the best alternative I had yet.

Once I had learnt all about the Compagnons and their way of life, it took me only a few moments to track down the addresses and phone numbers of Compagnon houses in Brittany, making a note of the next opening hours.

I was calling them the first chance I got, I decided—and this time, I wouldn't let Erwan elude me again.

That's how the next Monday after class, I spread my notes around me and called the three main organizations in charge of housing Compagnons. I hit the jackpot in Brest.

"Of course I know Erwan Kermarrec!" the woman in charge replied once I'd explained why I was calling. "He's a regular sponsor for our young *aspirants* and he often gives classes here."

I couldn't stop the wide grin that spread across my face.

"That's great! Do you think you could give me his phone number?"

I felt her hesitate. I bit at my nails while I waited anxiously for her to reply. I'd never been able to kick the habit.

"I'm not sure I can do that."

I'd been afraid of that, and I sighed in disappointment. Everyone was so unhelpful! Had keeping secrets become a national hobby in the last few days? When I was a kid, everyone knew everybody's business. Why couldn't I find someone who was a bit of a busybody, who would tell me what I wanted to know with no compunctions? If every historian had to deal with this kind of informant, history books would look a lot more like Swiss cheese . . .

I was being unfair. She was within her rights not to tell me. She didn't know me, after all.

"I understand," I told her, unable to hide my disappointment.

I'd been so close!

"But if you like, I could give him your phone number and ask him to call you back."

"Oh! Er . . ."

That had brought me up short. I'd never expected not to be the one to initiate contact. I wanted to be ready when I spoke to him.

But I also knew this could be my only chance to find Erwan.

I leapt at it. "Okay. Here's my number."

I gave her my cell phone number. She wrote it down and promised

Erwan would call me back. I thanked her and almost hung up before I thought of asking the one question that had been bothering me for so long.

"Do you know if he's married?"

"So is he?" Bérénice asked.

We'd gathered for our weekly knitting circle, and as had become my habit since the beginning of all this, I'd updated them on what I had found so far, to a backdrop of clicking needles.

"Not as far as she knew. And she didn't think he'd ever *been* married, either. Do you think maybe he never forgot Amélie?"

My phone rang before Angélique could do anything more than open her mouth to answer. I set my knitting aside and picked up.

"Can I speak to Ms. Richalet, please?"

The voice was deep, a little rasping.

"That's me."

"Good evening, I apologize for the inconvenience. This is Erwan Kermarrec."

"Oh. Oh! OH!"

I sat up and waved my arms haphazardly to catch my friends' attention, eyes wide, mouthing *Girls! It's him! It's Erwan!* They immediately froze and focused on me.

"Good evening, Mr. Kermarrec!"

I tried my best to sound cool and detached, which was not easy. I felt like a teenager with a crush, who'd just received a text from the boy of her dreams. I called upon my teaching experience to don the calm and serious expression I showed my students, before I went on.

"I'm so glad you called! It wasn't easy getting ahold of you."

"No, I don't suppose it was. Laurence, the woman you talked to when you called, told me you found a document mentioning my name?"

A straightforward kind of guy. No time to lose.

And I had a thousand questions to ask him, and just as many scenarios that I wanted to run by him . . . "In a way, yes. It's actually a letter. One you wrote."

There was silence on the other end of the line. When he spoke, I could tell from his voice that I had his full attention.

"I haven't written many letters over the course of my life."

"This one . . . This one never reached its intended recipient. I was the one who received it."

I explained that I lived in Karouac in the former principal's house. I felt him hesitate.

"How old is this letter?"

"It was written in 1971."

I held my breath. I heard him sigh, and he was silent for a long time.

"Mr. Kermarrec, are you there?"

"I am. It was a letter to Amélie, wasn't it?"

It hadn't taken him very long to understand what I was talking about. Did that mean that forty-five years later, he still thought of her?

"Yes," I answered eagerly.

"How . . . how did my letter fall into your hands?"

I briefly outlined what had happened: how the letter had arrived among a heap of bills and I had opened it, curious; how I'd tried to understand what had happened; how I'd retraced their steps and decided to find him. Find both of them.

Erwan listened in silence. Once I was finished, there was a slight quaver to his voice when he asked, "Both of us . . . Did you find Amélie too?"

"I did."

I'd even done one better. I hadn't told anyone yet, but just before I left home to head over to Le Fil d'Ariane, Chantale had called with Amélie's phone number and address.

My quest was nearly at its end.

"Have you spoken to her?" Erwan asked.

"Not yet. I haven't had the time. So she doesn't know about the letter."

"Very well. I know I don't really have the right to ask this of you, but is there any chance you'd be willing to return the letter to me without mentioning it to her?"

"Oh. Er . . . Sure," I said, somewhat taken aback.

I hadn't exactly planned for things to go this way, but it was his letter. I supposed he was entitled to have it back. "If you give me your address, I can mail it to you tomorrow."

"Do you have a pen and paper?"

"Wait a minute . . ."

I dug into my purse and extracted my notebook and pen. "I'm listening."

He spelled out an address in the Finistère and a phone number.

"All right, I'll post it tomorrow."

"Now that I think of it . . . I know this is asking a lot, but would you come and give it to me in person? I would hate to lose that letter again. Or I could come and get it, if you prefer. I know the place . . ."

"Oh! Oh. Er. No, it's fine, I can drive over and bring it along. It's not a problem."

I flicked through a mental calendar. Classes, end-of-year exams, grading . . . That would take me to early July, easy. Then there would be my father's birthday, his wedding anniversary, and the shop inventory that I'd promised to help out with, but I had a week-long gap before I had to tackle those. And I had to admit, nothing would please me more than spending a few days in the Finistère, like my father and I used to do when I was a little girl. Images of those days once again came back to me. The raw beauty of the region, where the sea crashed on the rocky cliffs, where little gray-stone houses bravely faced the winds and the sometimes violent tides, where lighthouses stood proud on rocks that looked like small islands, sending out their lights to guide ships safely to the shore. There, the sea reached so far to the horizon that it felt like the end of the world. And actually, it was in a sense, Brittany being the western-most region of France.

No, I thought to myself, *I really wouldn't mind going back there, even if it is only for a few days.*

"I can come over right before the fourteenth of July," I offered. "Can you wait until then? I'm afraid I won't be free before that."

"What are a few short weeks after forty-five years? Thank you for being willing to do this for me."

"You're very welcome. Could you recommend a hotel or bed-and-breakfast somewhere nearby? I think I'll make a holiday of it."

"I know just the place. I'll call and book for you."

"No need to go so out of your way."

"I insist. I am the one asking you to come this far, it seems like the least I can do. Don't worry, my nephew is the owner. It won't take but a minute."

"If you insist."

"Marvelous. Please give me a call when you know exactly what day you'll be coming, and I'll handle everything."

"Thank you so much. I'll phone you back as soon as possible."

"Goodbye, Ms. Richalet."

"Flavie," I said, on autopilot. "Goodbye, Mr. Kermarrec."

"Please call me Erwan, then."

"All right, Erwan. Goodbye."

I hung up, slightly dizzy from the speed at which everything had fallen into place. My friends had followed the conversation eagerly. Well—what they could hear of it.

"Girls, I think I've found Erwan at last."

Karouac, Brittany
August 31, 1971

It was his last evening in Karouac.

They met on the beach, at the same place they'd met every night for the past seven weeks. The surrounding rocks cut the small creek off from the rest of the world.

It had been here that they had danced by moonlight, here that they had spent hours talking about everything and nothing, their projects, their dreams, here that they had kissed for the first time . . .

She was gazing at the ocean while she waited for him. The sky was clear, and pale moonlight pooled over the sand.

He drew closer and wordlessly closed his arms around her, hugging her to him, so tight it was as though he wanted her to sink through his skin and nestle in his heart forever.

After what seemed like a lifetime, he stepped away and their eyes met.

"Amélie, I—"

"Shh," she interrupted, her finger on his lips. "You don't have to say anything. I don't want you to promise me anything. I love you, Erwan, too much to try to pin you down with promises you may not be able to keep."

"I love you, Amélie. More than anything else in this world."

Sadness crept into her eyes when he said this. "Then write to me whenever you can, if you will. Come back when you can, when you're able to. Don't forget me."

"Never. I'd never forget you, Amélie. My precious Lili."

There were tears in her eyes, but she did not blink. She gazed at him for several long seconds, before she leaned forward and kissed him lightly, sweetly. There were tear tracks on her face and he could feel a tang of salt on her lips. His heart broke and shattered into a thousand pieces. He clung to her, his hands coming up to frame her face and hold her near.

He didn't want to go. Not anymore.

When he felt her draw back he opened his eyes. She unbuttoned her shirt, and shimmied out of her skirt, letting it fall onto the sand, her eyes never leaving his. Only then did Erwan notice the picnic blanket she'd spread out at their feet. His gaze traveled up her naked legs, sliding over her underwear, her flat belly, her breasts still hidden by the bra she was unclasping. Her pale skin was bathed in moonlight, and she looked unreal, like some otherworldly goddess. His goddess.

His heart was beating fit to burst. Somehow, it still found a way to speed up when Amélie lowered her bra, stepped out of her underwear. Utterly naked, she came to him and started to unbutton his shirt.

She never looked away.

Erwan left at dawn the next day with a heavy heart. The sun was barely out and most birds were still asleep.

He'd arrived on September first and he was leaving again exactly one year later. But he wasn't the same man anymore. He had completely changed. Amélie had changed him.

Amélie, whom he'd left on the beach just moments before, the taste of her tearstained farewell kiss still on his lips. He'd asked her not to go with him to the bus stop. He'd rather keep the memory of her on the beach, her hair loose and a blanket wrapped around her naked body. That would be easier.

Or so he'd thought.

The bus doors swung open. Erwan got to his feet and hefted his bag up. Then he turned and looked over his shoulder toward the town, toward the beach. Toward her.

"Are you coming?" the bus driver griped. "I haven't got all day!"

"Yes, I'm coming."

With one last look, one last whisper of a goodbye, he got on the bus and let it take him away to the next part of his life.

La Rochelle.

Chapter 7

I drove into Port-l'Abbé on July eleventh under a blazing sun. The trip from Karouac had been quite easy, thanks to the GPS Cécile had loaned me. I left home early in the morning, the sun already high in the sky, driving with all the windows open, singing loudly with the radio. Because I had time, instead of the shorter, faster, but less interesting route, I chose to take the long way around, the one that would take me through miles and miles of agricultural fields and through many a cute little country village, complete with cobbled streets, pointy churches, and half-timbered or gray-stone houses that were typical of Brittany—and through the wonderful and magical Armorique natural park. I've always loved that place, regretting that it was a bit too far from home to be able to go there to write my books. I always felt inspired there. Maybe it was because of the legends that filled the air, maybe it was the quiet, the calm, the serenity that oozes from every tree, every leaf, every breath of the wind. Or maybe because it has some kind of magical feeling to it, like you could almost feel the fairies flying around you, hear the korrigans—Breton fairy sorceresses—laugh under the rocks.

There was a place in this park, a belvedere at the top of a hill, where you could see the most wonderful panorama of the region, with all its diversity and its beauty: forest, country, rivers, all the colors mixing to create the most beautiful landscape. Some days, when the weather was clear, you could even get a glimpse of the sea, where the horizon met the sky.

That day, I could.

In anticipation, I had bought a small picnic at a nice bakery just before driving through the park. After parking my car, I hiked up the hill with my sandwich and cookie, and ate in silence, sitting on a rock, my eyes to the west, on the forest and the sea far beyond, remembering the stories and legends my father told me the first time we came, as we watched the clouds cast shadows and play with the colors of the forest, the fields, and the river surrounding the hill.

And I listened closely, like he told me that time.

And when I left the place an hour later, I had a smile on my face: I had felt the fairies whisper their secrets in my ears.

That smile didn't leave me the rest of the short trip to my destination.

Port-l'Abbé was a typical Breton sea-facing town, quite similar to Karouac, actually, though much smaller, with a narrow main street and even narrower secondary ones, all cobbled at the center of the village, and two-story half-timbered buildings with colorful windows that rapidly gave way to family houses with flower gardens. It was only a matter of moments before I pulled up to a cottage surrounded by a rather large garden and a high hedge just by the sea, a few miles out of town.

I parked in front and gave my father a quick call to tell him I'd arrived safely, with no accidents or serial-killer hitchhikers along the way. I typed a brief e-mail to the knitting circle to tell them more or less the same thing, then I stepped out of the car and, shouldering my purse, I went up to the garden gate. I rang and waited for Erwan to open, my heart beating double time.

Nothing.

I rang again. Still nothing.

Damn. Was I too early? *Maybe I should have called ahead and told him precisely what time I was coming.* I grimaced. Over the phone, I had only told him the day I would arrive, but not the time. What was I going to do if he wasn't home? I didn't even know where his nephew's bed-and-breakfast was, so I couldn't drop off my bags in the meantime . . . *I could always go for a walk on the beach,* I thought as I rang a third time.

To no effect. What now?

The gate was unlatched. I hesitated for a moment, then I let myself in and went around to the back of the house, thinking maybe Erwan was in the garden and had failed to hear the bell.

There was indeed someone in the backyard. Or rather, two someones. Two wide-shouldered, muscular silhouettes, one of them leaning over a magnificent rosebush and the other pulling up a few weeds bold enough to try to grow between two glorious rhododendrons.

I hitched my purse higher on my shoulder, fluffed my hair, and cleared my throat.

"Mr. Kermarrec? Erwan?"

Both of them turned around as one. Their resemblance struck me immediately. They were both impressively tall and broad-shouldered, they had the same square jaw, the same wild hair, though one's was salt-and-pepper and the other's was jet black, down to the same expression on their faces. Even their eyes were almost identical. Erwan's—for it had to be him—were a clear gray, while the other man's—I could only guess he was the nephew Erwan had mentioned—were a cerulean blue so deep and intense they were almost mesmerizing.

I tried to control the fluttering of my heart, which definitely sped up when I met Erwan's nephew's gaze. He was almost too good-looking, his eyes stunning.

I diverted my eyes, focusing on his uncle instead. He hadn't changed much from the photo I'd found, even though forty-five years had gone by. Time had left its mark on him, that much was undeniable, but his eyes belonged to the young man in the photograph. His face still had a shy, warm, and kind expression. There was no doubt about it. This was the man I had spent so many weeks looking for.

"That's me," he confirmed.

The words made me dizzy with glee. It felt as though I'd met Santa Claus in the flesh, along with the Easter bunny, the tooth fairy, and the king of Candy Land. My quest was finally at its end. I had found Erwan, and he was exactly as I'd pictured him.

A huge smile made its way across my face, and before I realized what I was doing, I threw myself at him and hugged him with all the strength in my body.

"I'm so glad to finally meet you in the flesh. You cannot imagine how long I've been thinking about you!"

"Well, I wasn't expecting quite so enthusiastic a greeting." Erwan laughed, looking slightly embarrassed. "But it is kind of you."

I stepped back immediately, my face burning. "I'm so sorry. I have no idea what came over me. I've been picturing this meeting for such a long time I kind of lost touch with reality. I'm really sorry."

"Don't apologize. It's been a while since a beautiful woman embraced me. Except for my niece, of course. When you're my age, you don't get women flinging themselves at you every day."

I smiled when he tried to downplay my embarrassing greeting. He was still slightly uncomfortable, I could tell. He was a gentleman, and he tried not to make a big deal of it so things wouldn't get too awkward. I didn't think there were many men these days who'd be so thoughtful toward a perfect stranger.

That was when his nephew stepped forward and met my gaze. His voice was low and warm, and it made me shiver all over.

"Hi, I'm Romaric. Can I offer you a drink?"

In a matter of moments, I was sitting under a tree, chatting with Romaric—who not only was devastatingly handsome, but also had a *very* sexy name. Once we'd been introduced, Erwan suggested I sit on the terrace while he put his gardening tools away. Romaric had been given the task of entertaining me in the meantime.

He set to his duties with zeal. "Did you have a nice trip?" he asked.

"I did, thank you. No aliens, no serial killers. No farmers' protest either, so I guess it falls under the heading of a good trip. I even stopped for a bit of sightseeing."

Romaric laughed and I melted inside.

Even the sound of his laughter was sexy. *Dear God.*

"Never miss an opportunity for sightseeing."

"My thoughts exactly!"

"Erwan told me you're from Karouac. I don't know where that is."

"In the Côtes-d'Armor, next to Lannion. It's a charming little town, or at least that's what the entrance sign would have you believe. Five thousand inhabitants, little stone houses, flower-filled gardens. It is a lovely rural Breton town. I'm sure you can visualize what I'm talking about."

"Indeed I can." He grinned.

"It's a beautiful town," I went on, "and I fell in love with it as soon as I moved there."

He smiled, and it felt like the sun was shining on me. "Most towns in Brittany are that way. You come, you get attached, you stay . . ."

"You're right. That's the beauty of it."

We just looked at each other for a few moments, little smiles on both our faces, before Romaric glanced away.

"And, er, what do you do in this 'charming little town'?" He jabbed air quotes with his fingers.

"For a living, you mean?"

He nodded.

"I teach history and geography in Lannion."

I braced myself for the *You must have lots of holidays!* that people often say. To my great surprise, he simply nodded.

"I admire people who make a career out of teaching, like you. I don't think I'd have the patience."

"It's not a question of patience so much as love."

"Love?"

"Love of history, of the past, a willingness to hand that legacy down to future generations. Or at least"—I laughed self-consciously—"that's the way I see it. But it feels like kids are growing wilder by the year, and utterly uninterested in history. I try my best to make it feel real to them, but sometimes . . . it's just not enough. And occasionally they have their own problems, and they have other concerns which trump their studies, and I can't do anything about that."

"That must be hard."

"It is, kind of. But let's not be depressing on a beautiful day." I deliberately switched to a more cheerful tone. "Let's talk about something else. You run a bed-and-breakfast?"

"A few minutes' drive away. You probably passed it on your way here. I do rent out rooms and also lead horseback rides around Port-l'Abbé."

"You mean that gorgeous cottage with a huge garden where I saw two magnificent horses munching away on the lawn?"

He laughed again. "That's the one!"

"Well, I seem to have lucked out! That looks pretty cozy."

Over the next few minutes, Romaric told me about the bed-and-breakfast and how he'd opened it with his younger sister a few years back. He explained how it worked, how they hosted riders and their horses, and organized their own horseback rides. Usually his sister, Gwenn, led those, but from time to time he got into the saddle.

"I've only gone riding a couple of times in my life," I admitted. "And that was a long time ago, but I'm sure it must be great to go for a ride in the woods or on the beach."

"You could take Flavie, Rom," Erwan suggested, and I jumped, startled.

Chapter 8

We'd been so deep in conversation that I hadn't heard Ewan approach. I wondered how long he'd been listening.

"Oh please, I don't want to be any more of a bother than I already am," I protested feebly, even though hearing Romaric talk about his horses had given me an irresistible urge to learn how to ride.

"If you'd like to, it's easy enough to work out," Romaric said at once. "Just say the word, and we can find a time to do it."

"Well . . . If you're sure it isn't too much trouble, I'd love to!"

"That's settled, then. Gwenn's pretty busy these days, so you'll probably have to ride with me, if you don't mind."

"Of course not!" *Oh boy, I don't mind at all.* I blushed.

Romaric's only answer was to give me one of those brilliant smiles, and I almost felt the earth shake beneath my feet.

How peculiar.

Erwan sat next to me, and Romaric poured him a glass of juice.

"You ride too?" I asked Erwan.

"Not as much as I used to, but I was a decent rider back in the day."

"Don't you miss it?"

"I do, but these old bones wouldn't stand for it anymore."

"Erwan, you're still young," I said.

"It's nice of you to say so, even if it's patently untrue."

We made some small talk for a few more minutes. Then I took advantage of a lull in the conversation to draw the letter from my purse and hand it to Erwan.

"Here. You've waited long enough. You must be eager to get it back."

Something strange welled up inside me when I let go of the letter, relinquishing it to its true owner. A mix of excitement from my search coming to its end and regret at having to give it back. It felt like a chapter in my life was closing. For weeks, I'd been a part of Erwan and Amélie's story, trying to find out what had happened, to connect the pieces I'd unearthed. And now here I was, returning the letter to its sender. It had never reached the addressee, and I still didn't know exactly what had happened.

I wasn't sure whether I'd be able to convince Erwan to tell me his story.

It was like turning the last page of a book and finding the author had left the ending unfinished.

But even though I was returning the letter to its true owner, I wasn't turning over a new leaf just yet. Before I'd slipped the letter into my purse the day before, I copied it down in my notebook next to the two articles I'd taped there and all the notes I'd jotted down over the course of the last few weeks. I knew I didn't need it—each word, each comma had been branded into my memory—but I couldn't stand the idea of not having it with me any longer. I'd even managed to convince myself that it was purely for the sake of research for my future novel that I was copying it down. I'd always been quite good at telling myself what I wanted to hear. But the truth was that it was a way of keeping a piece of their story with me, of not saying good-bye just yet.

I used to hate goodbyes. I still do, but I'm better at them these days.

Wordlessly, Erwan grasped the letter very lightly, as though he was afraid he'd damage it.

"Thank you," he said, lifting it up and turning it over, but making no move to unfold it.

Romaric turned to me. "You received this in the mail, is that it?"

"Yes. Incredible as it seems, it was in some drawer for the last forty-five years. And when it finally arrived, I was the one who received it instead of the intended person."

"That's unbelievable!"

"But true . . ."

"And with just a letter, you were able to find Erwan?" Romaric asked.

"Trust me, it was no easy task!" I outlined my search, omitting the leads that hadn't panned out. I explained about Chantale and the newspaper articles, and how I'd met with Father François—"He wants to hear from you," I told Erwan—and how I'd phoned the Compagnons' lodge in Brest.

"So you haven't spoken to Amélie?"

"No."

I'd been dying to, but I hadn't dared call her once I'd agreed to give the letter back to Erwan. What could I tell her? *Hi, I've received a letter addressed to you, a wedding proposal that never found its way to you, but I'm about to give it back to your old flame, so I guess you still won't be reading it today! Bye!*

There was no way I could do that. So I hadn't reached out to her, though it broke my heart.

"But you have her number," Romaric said.

"I do." I turned to Erwan. "Do you want it?"

There was a flash of pain in his eyes, and I wondered if maybe I shouldn't have offered.

He stared at me for a long while, and I could see the indecision in his face. Then he shook his head and looked back down at the letter, still in its envelope.

"It's too late. She's married, anyway."

"She got divorced," I couldn't help but add before I bit my lip.

One day, my recklessness would be the ruin of me. Or it would hurt someone else, which would be worse.

Erwan's head snapped up, and for a second, I thought he'd changed his mind. But in the end, he just shook his head again. "It was such a long time ago. It's too late now."

"Erwan—" Romaric began, but his phone rang at the same moment, and he looked at the screen. "It's Gwenn. Excuse me."

He moved away, and I leaned forward and touched Erwan's shoulder, unable to resist a final plea. "If you ever change your mind, I'll be happy to give you her phone number."

I saw in his face then how tempted he was, how much he wanted to say yes. But resignation replaced it so fast I doubted what I'd seen.

"Thank you, Flavie, but . . ."

"But?"

"Never mind. Thank you for coming all this way to bring this letter. It means a lot to me."

"You're welcome," I said softly. "I'm glad I could help."

"I'm sorry, Gwenn needs me at the bed-and-breakfast," Romaric said as he came back toward us. "Do you want to come and check in, Flavie?"

"That would be great, thanks." I stood up. "Erwan, can I come back later? There's something I'd like to talk about with you."

"In that case, would you like to have dinner with me tonight?"

"I can't think of anything that would please me more."

"Seven o'clock?"

"It's a date, then!"

Once Flavie had left, Erwan went back to the terrace and sat down, still holding the letter.

Amélie had never received it.

Amélie, his Lili . . .

That explained so much. Her absence. Her silence.

What had she thought when she'd received nothing for weeks? Had she believed he'd forgotten her, forgotten what they'd promised each other that day on the beach?

How many times, over the past forty-five years, had he wondered why she'd never written back? Why had he not thought that his letter had gone astray? That she might never have received it? He'd thought of every possibility except that one.

Except that one . . .

Why had he been so stupid? He should have gone to Paris when he'd learned she'd left Karouac. He should have told her mother how important Amélie was to him, and that he hoped she would give her daughter the message that he'd called. He should have looked beyond his wounded pride and convinced her to give him Amélie's number. He should have done all that was in his power to prove to Amélie how much he loved her, that he was good enough for her, that she was the one for him.

He should never have waited.

That had been his greatest mistake, one he'd regretted ever since he'd learned the letter had never made its way to her.

He leaned back in his chair and closed his eyes, reliving the memory of that phone call for the thousandth time.

La Rochelle
October 1971

In the small inn by the port, Erwan listened as the phone rang, his heart beating with a mixture of anxiety, uncertainty, and impatience.

Five weeks. Five weeks he'd been waiting patiently, every evening, for a sign that she had come to find him. At first he hadn't worried. He'd expected some delay in which she'd receive the letter and write back, maybe a week. But a fortnight had passed, then three weeks, four, five, and he'd grown worried. He didn't know what her silence meant. So he'd decided to call.

"Hello?"

A woman's voice. Erwan took a deep breath.

"Hello, is this Mrs. Lacombe?"

"Yes. What can I do for you?"

"Can I speak to Amélie, please?"

His heart was beating double time, and his hands shook. He'd never spoken to her parents before.

"I'm sorry, Amélie isn't here. Who is this?"

"I'm . . . I'm a friend of hers."

"A friend?"

"Yes, a friend. My name's Erwan. Do you know when she'll be home?"

"Home? She's living in Paris now, she's studying there."

It was like being hit in the face. In Paris? What . . . How . . . Why hadn't she told him on their last day together that she'd managed to convince her parents to let her go to Paris? He didn't understand. He needed to speak to her.

"Do you have a phone number I could call?"

"Young man, you seem like a nice person, but I don't know you, and I'm certainly not going to hand out my daughter's phone number to a stranger."

Erwan closed his eyes as pain lanced through him. Of course. Her mother wouldn't know him. Amélie had never mentioned him.

"All right. I understand. Could you . . . Could you tell her I called, next time you speak to her? Can I give you my address?"

"Let me grab a pen. Okay, I'm listening."

He rattled off his name and the address of the inn he'd given in his letter, the one where he'd begged Amélie to meet him.

He would never have been so bold, had not Sophie, the inn's owner, offered to help. They had become friends shortly after he had arrived in La Rochelle. He was working on the port, on the restoration of an old building nearby, and day after day, as he was eating his lunch alone, his sad eyes gazing toward the sea, remembering the feeling of her, the touch of her, the smell of her, the way her body fitted perfectly into his, Sophie had watched him from afar. Until one day, she came to speak to him. She was so kind, so understanding, that before he knew it, he was telling her of his broken heart, of his longing, of the dreams he hadn't even dared admit to himself yet. "If you love her that much, tell her," she had said. That's when a plan had started to form into his mind. He had asked Sophie if she would help him, and she said yes, she would help any way she could. So, filled with hope, he had written the letter, and begged Amélie to meet him at the inn—he couldn't very well set the rendezvous point at the Compagnon house where he was living. Sophie had promised to let him know as soon as Amélie arrived.

But she never came.

"Please tell her I'll be there until after Christmas," Erwan said. "Tell her . . ."

Tell her I miss her so much I can barely breathe. That when she's away, the days are dull, that she's my sunshine and that I can't, won't, live without her, he wanted to scream into the phone.

But he stayed silent. He couldn't say that to Amélie's mother. She'd think he was crazy for sure.

"Just tell her I'll wait for her to call or write. Whatever she wants," he said in the end.

He thanked her and hung up with a heavy heart.

In Karouac, Viviane Lacombe set the phone down and tore the sheet of paper from the notepad where she'd written the young man's name and address. She put it away in a drawer. She made a note to herself to mention it in her next letter to her daughter.

But fate was against Erwan, and decided otherwise. A few days later, Amélie's father went through the drawers, throwing away papers that had been lying around for too long. He never even looked at the precious note as it went straight into the trash.

And Erwan continued to wait for a call that would never come.

Chapter 9

"Erwan, that was absolutely delicious!" I exclaimed as I swallowed the last strawberry on my plate later that evening.

"Care for another helping?"

"I'd love one, but I think I'd explode if I took one more mouthful."

"Coffee? Tea?" he offered.

"Maybe in half an hour?"

"I'll ask again then."

I leaned back in my chair, looked up, and took a deep breath.

We were sitting on the terrace as the sun slowly sank below the horizon. The heat of the day had subsided, and a cool evening breeze was bringing the scent of salt and seaweed from the beach. It felt very peaceful.

I was on holiday, and I was starting to feel the tension I'd collected during the school year slowly leave the muscles in my neck, back, and shoulders.

As planned, I walked over to Erwan's after I'd unpacked at the bed-and-breakfast. We spent the entire evening chatting. Though I'd known him for only a few hours, I already enjoyed his company immensely. He was a deeply kind and generous man, both open-minded and welcoming. A real gentleman like in the old days, with impeccable manners. How many men drew back a woman's chair before she sat down at the table?

If he hadn't been old enough to be my father at the very least, I think I could have fallen in love with his kindness and gentleness. I no longer had any doubts as to whether Amélie had been truly in love with him. I was even ready to bet he'd been a regular heartthrob during his younger years.

"You haven't told me whether you liked Romaric and Gwenn's bed-and-breakfast," Erwan said, interrupting my thoughts on his character. "How is it?"

"It's perfect. So beautiful. I actually don't have the words to express how much I love it."

And no, I was not biased by the fact that his handsome and sexy nephew owned it. From the moment I had set foot there, the entire area exuded a sense of peace that appealed to me. On one side, the sea was a few hundred meters from the stables; on the other, a trail led straight to the woods. The whole place felt like an island of peace and quiet. I hadn't gone up to the horses' corral yet, but it was several dozen meters long and ran along the left side of the house.

I'd fallen in love with the place before I even stepped into Le Haras, as Romaric's bed-and-breakfast was called, but what I saw inside finished the job.

Wainscoting layered the lower half of the walls, and the upper half was painted a clear, crisp white. One wall in the entrance was covered with dozens of photographs of Romaric and his sister riding various horses. On the left, a staircase led up to the second floor, while a vast living room connecting through an open arch to the kitchen lay on the right. Light streamed through a couple of huge bay windows into both rooms. Outside were a terrace and a swimming pool. I was impressed by the size of the place; it was much larger than it seemed from the outside. It was also warm and welcoming, and I had told Romaric so. It was very cozy, and I had felt instantly at home.

"Romaric and your niece—her name is Gwenn, right?" Erwan nodded. "They really went all out to make it feel like home; I already know I'm going to enjoy my stay very much. And by the way, thank you so much for booking it for me. That was really sweet of you."

"Don't mention it. I told Romaric that you were coming and there was a vacancy. No problem at all."

I tried to dig a little deeper.

"You're close with your nephew and niece, aren't you?"

"They're like my children. Their parents were killed in a car crash some twenty years ago, and I became their legal guardian."

"Oh my God! That must have been so difficult for them."

"It was. Romaric was only a teenager, with his own set of problems. Gwenn was barely ten. It was a difficult adjustment period for them."

"For you as well, I imagine. Are they your brother's children?"

"My younger brother, yes."

"They were lucky to have you. At least they didn't end up in foster care."

"That was the one thing I wanted to avoid at all costs. I fought for them to be allowed to stay with me. I wasn't married, so it was a difficult case, but I won in the end."

"You never married later on?"

"No."

Silence fell for a few moments, and for the thousandth time in less than a month, I wondered if the feelings he'd had—and maybe still did—for Amélie were the reason he'd stayed single.

"Did you never meet the right person?"

"Oh, but I did. And I was a fool to let her get away."

I hesitated for a few seconds, then went ahead. "Can I ask you something? And please feel free to tell me if this makes you uncomfortable, or you'd rather not speak of it," I added immediately. "You can tell me to get lost, okay?"

"All right. What is it?"

"It's not actually a question, more of a request. I . . . I was wondering whether you'd tell me your story. What happened with Amélie."

"You know, it's not that exciting a story. We met, we loved each other for one brief, amazing summer, then life took us on different paths. Not exactly novel-worthy."

"Well . . ."

"Well what?"

"I think it is."

"How so?"

"Sometimes when I'm not teaching, I write. Fiction, a couple of novels. And I was wondering—well, hoping actually—that you'd let me write your story. About how you met Amélie."

"You do realize it doesn't have a happy ending?"

For now, I thought.

"I do," I said. "But I thought I'd change the ending so you—well, the hero, really—finds her again. If you agree, of course."

"And you'd publish it?"

"Yes, but I would make sure to change all the names, so that your privacy would be protected. No one would know that you were my inspiration."

"I see."

"So . . . are you willing?" I asked shyly.

"Well . . . I don't see why not."

"You know," he said a few moments later, handing me a steaming cup of tea, "I've never told anybody about Amélie. You'll be the first."

"Not even your nephew and niece?"

"No." He sipped his cup of coffee. "There never really was an opportunity. It was old news by the time they were born, and I never thought about sharing it with them."

"Will you, one day?"

"If they want to know, of course I will. It's not as though it's a secret. It's just a tale of young love."

I smiled and kept silent. I was sure that it was much, much more.

He leaned back in his chair, setting his cup on the table in front of him, and began.

"The first time I saw her was at the Bastille Day dance in 1971. Almost forty-five years ago to the day. She was wearing a deep red dress, and she was the most beautiful woman I'd ever seen . . ."

Over the next hour, Erwan told me everything. How they'd met at the party, how they'd spent their evenings on the beach. How he loved her, and how much it had hurt when he'd had to leave.

How, missing her fiercely, he'd written that letter to her, on the advice of the inn's owner, whom he had befriended while working on the port. How he'd called a few weeks later, driven mad with longing. Waiting, again, never hearing from her. Then, finally giving up, deciding to pursue his own life and go on his Tour de France, the journey across France that every aspiring Compagnon has to go through at the end of his training. And how he'd returned a few years later—stumbling upon her marrying another man, breaking his heart for the second time without even knowing it.

I listened wordlessly, letting the words sink in, feeling as though I was experiencing the younger Erwan's every emotion. I couldn't hold back the tears that welled up when he told me about his conversation with Amélie's mother. One of them slid down my cheek when I pictured the scene at the church.

It was such a shame. They'd been so close to happily-ever-after. It had been just one letter away . . .

"I should have insisted more." There was regret in Erwan's voice. "When I received no answer, I should have tried harder to find her, interrupted my journey as long as was necessary in order to find her and convince her."

"Why didn't you?" I tried to control the tremor in my voice.

I had never been so moved by a story. I may have cried on occasion—okay, often—when writing particularly sad or moving scenes, but I had never been so sad.

Why had life kept them apart?

"Pride, I suppose. Misplaced and utterly unjustified pride. I was hurt she hadn't told her parents about me. I was disappointed she hadn't tried to find me, that she hadn't kept her promise that she'd wait for me as long as necessary. I started to think that maybe I'd only been a passing fancy for her. That her promises were only spur-of-the-moment. That she didn't want to see me anymore and that keeping silent was her way of telling me so . . .

"I never thought that maybe she had not received my letter. And now I wonder whether her mother remembered to tell her I'd called. I don't know. I don't know what happened to her, what she thought or felt. All I know is that maybe if I had proved to her that I loved her, if I had insisted a little more, she wouldn't have married that man. So in the end, it is my own fault. I didn't deserve her."

"Don't say that. Of course you deserved her. You still do!"

"It's too late."

I stayed silent for a few moments. "You still love her, don't you?" It was more of a statement than a question.

"I never stopped loving her. Even when I was hurt and angry, when I thought she hadn't kept her promise to wait for me, she never stopped being the one and only woman for me. I still think about her every day."

I could feel my heart shattering into a thousand pieces. Forty-five years later, and he still loved her as much as he had on the day they'd met. Despite years spent apart, he still loved her with all his heart.

I had to do something. I couldn't stand the idea that he was so unhappy when maybe . . . Maybe Amélie was still in love with him too.

I had to find her. I couldn't leave things as they were. If I had even the slightest chance of reuniting Erwan and Amélie, I had to seize it.

A plan was starting to come together in my mind.

I knew what I was going to do.

"It's never too late," I offered cautiously. "A love like yours is both precious and rare. It's never too late to fight for it. Like my father used to say, everything can be changed. Only death is forever. And even that is negotiable. Just look at Orpheus."

Erwan's smile was infinitely sad. "You are young, Flavie. One day you may learn that love is not always enough to overcome all the obstacles in your way."

"I do know, Erwan." I sighed. "It wasn't enough for my mother."

"Your mother?"

Now it was my turn to unearth an old story no one knew, not even the knitting circle, though they were my closest friends. It was my own hidden wound.

And it probably was one of the reasons, if not *the* main reason, that I wished so hard for Amélie and Erwan to find each other again.

"My mother left when I was five. She left me and my father. I remember she was crying as she said that she loved us very much but that staying in Lannion was suffocating her, that she wanted more out of life, that she deserved more. It broke my father's heart. He never remarried, because he never forgot her. We never heard from her again. She never called for my birthday or even sent a card. She wasn't there when I graduated. She just walked out of our lives."

"That must have been extremely difficult to live through."

"For years I hated her. I resented what she'd done to us. And I couldn't understand why. How could she have just left without looking back? How can you pretend you love your family and just walk away with no regrets? That's when I understood that love isn't always enough."

"I'm so sorry you had to experience such pain."

"It's in the past now. I made my peace with it, and I don't hate her anymore. I just don't think about her. But I know my father still suffers over it, even twenty-five years later. And I can't do a thing to help him. But I can help *you*, Erwan. It's not too late!"

"Anybody home?" A woman's voice interrupted from around the corner of the house.

"We're over here!" Erwan called back, keeping his gaze trained on mine. "Listen, I'll think about it," he added in a lower tone. "I promise you that much."

"Thank you," I whispered back.

"What are you promising, Erwan?" the young woman asked as she rounded the corner.

She was around my age with bright, curly auburn hair. She smiled, and even if I hadn't seen the photos in the B & B, I would immediately have known who she was. Like with her brother, the resemblance to Erwan was too obvious to be missed.

"Gwenn, this is Flavie." Erwan gestured at me as he rose to kiss her cheek.

"Hello, Flavie! Sorry I missed you earlier; I was in the middle of something in the stables. I was cleaning the stalls and I thought you'd rather wait until I showered to introduce myself."

"That was thoughtful of you, thank you." I laughed.

"Romaric's just behind me, he was on the phone. Oh, here he comes."

There he was indeed. Almost instinctively, our gazes met. He smiled, and once again, I could have sworn I felt the earth quake beneath my feet.

Wow.

"Hi," he said.

"Hi," I parroted back, blinking stupidly.

Well, we certainly weren't in the running for wittiest conversation of the year.

"So what *were* you promising, Erwan?" Gwenn insisted.

"Curiosity killed the cat, haven't you heard?" Erwan teased her.

"Funnily enough, I have, and sometimes as much as five times a day. But apparently satisfaction brought it back. So?"

"I owe Flavie a dance at the Bastille Day party."

I raised an eyebrow at Erwan, and he winked at me.

Apparently I had a date.

* * *

I clicked immediately with Gwenn, as much as I had with Erwan and Romaric a few hours earlier, and the rest of the evening passed in a flash. The four of us talked a lot, about everything and nothing at the same time, about local legends, and being a teacher, about Port-l'Abbé and Karouac, about horses and animals in general, and other things. We joked too, and laughed. And as a companionable, easy silence fell, I realized that in that moment, I felt more at ease with these people I barely knew than I had with colleagues that I had worked with and known for years.

It was strange.

It was unusual.

I kind of loved it.

The sun had finally set, and the day had given way to a moonless night so dark that even with the solar lamps that Erwan had set up all around the terrace, I could barely see the faces of my companions. In the pitch-black sky, millions of stars were scintillating like diamonds. In the distance, I could hear the waves crashing onto the cliffs.

It felt peaceful, serene, relaxing. Beautiful.

Suddenly, I wanted time to stop, and I wanted to never leave this place.

"It's really nice here," I said softly, when nobody spoke. "The house *and* the village, I mean."

"It is," two male voices answered simultaneously.

Erwan and Romaric let out a laugh, and Gwenn and I chuckled with them.

"Karouac is a nice place too," Erwan added.

"Yes, it is, indeed," I agreed with a smile. "Have you been living here for long?"

"Forever," Erwan answered. "I bought the house not long after I finished my Tour de France. It's been home ever since."

Romaric joined in. "For us too. Even more than the bed-and-breakfast, this house has been and always will be our home. We have so many happy memories here . . ."

At that moment, the wind coming from the sea started blowing stronger, and I shivered with cold.

Immediately, Romaric took off his jacket.

"Here, take this," he said, as he set it lightly on my shoulders, his hands lingering a bit longer, the light touch of his fingers brushing my skin, making me tremble even more.

A strange feeling suddenly rushed through me, all over me, inside and out. A feeling of warmth, of . . . of home, in some strange way—with a pinch of sensuality suddenly gathering into the core of my body.

Of its own accord, my heart started beating faster, harder against my ribs, and goose bumps appeared all over my skin.

"Thank you," I said softly, flustered, hoping he wouldn't notice. Maybe it was a good thing that it was so dark. At least he couldn't see me blush. And neither could Erwan and Gwenn, which suited me just fine.

I slipped my hands into the sleeves, bringing the front of the jacket closer to me. I wasn't *that* cold, but some part of me couldn't resist. It felt warm, felt like . . . him. It was like being in his arms, without actually *being* in his arms. For a few seconds, eyes closed, breathing deep, I indulged myself in the lingering scent of him, the feeling of him, as images of his arms around me, his body against mine, suddenly rushed into my mind. My cheeks went from warm to scorching hot, and it was all I could do not to put my cold hands on my warm face, tipping them off about what I had been thinking.

Stop that, I said to myself, as my mind started to offer vivid images of his hands burrowing in my hair, and his lips kissing the soft skin of my neck. *Stop that right now! You've only just met him! What's come over you all of a sudden?*

I cleared my throat, trying to act as though his gesture didn't affect me at all.

"Thank you," I repeated more firmly, "that's very kind of you. Very gentlemanly," I added, teasing.

"You are very welcome. I was raised well," he answered, and in the darkness, his eyes seemed to gleam.

My heart skipped a beat, and butterflies gathered in my stomach.

"Anyway, I should be going," I said, standing up and burying my hands into the pockets of his jacket in order to avoid jumping into his arms. "It's getting late and I need my beauty sleep."

"Do you want us to drive you back to the B and B?" Romaric offered.

Yes! I wanted to scream. *I'd love you to!*

"Well, I wouldn't say no, if it's no bother to you," I said circumspectly. "I don't want you to leave on my account."

"Absolutely not. I need to get up early, so I should be going too."

"Then I'll gladly accept your offer."

"Gwenn, are you ready to go too?" Romaric asked, turning to his sister.

"I am," she said, drinking the last drop in her glass. "I have things to do in the morning too."

"Well, if everyone is leaving," Erwan said, standing up, "I'll be heading to bed too. My old bones aren't used to staying up late."

"You keep saying that you're old, but you're not, Erwan," I said.

"And that's not true, but thank you for saying so." He smiled, opening his arms so I could hug him goodbye.

And this time, hugging him felt natural.

As if he was family.

"Thank you for having me," I said. "The food was delicious."

"It's you I should thank, for keeping me company tonight. And for bringing me back that letter."

"You are very welcome, Erwan. It was my pleasure."

"You'll have to show it to us one day, Erwan!" Gwenn teased, hugging her uncle goodbye too. "After all, if Flavie got to read it, we should too!"

"Maybe, if you behave."

"I never behave. You should know that by now."

"I do know."

"But you'll show it to me anyway," Gwenn added, a smile on her lips, "because you cannot refuse me anything."

"The worst part of it all is that you are right, I cannot refuse you anything."

"I know!"

I smiled. I loved the way they interacted, teasing each other with love and kindness. I wish I could have had brothers and sisters like them. I had the girls, though, and they were like family to me. Thinking of the knitting circle reminded me that I needed to write my friends, as soon as possible, to let them know what I learned tonight. They were probably dying of curiosity by now.

"See you soon?" Erwan asked, turning to me, interrupting my train of thought.

"Of course. Remember, you owe me a dance!" I joked.

"I can't wait," he said with a smile.

Then it was Romaric's turn to kiss his uncle good-night. "See you tomorrow, Erwan. I'll come as soon as I can tomorrow to finish the garden with you."

"All right, I'll wait for you."

"Perfect." Romaric turned to me. "Are you ready to go, Flavie?"

"I am. Good night, Erwan. And think of what I said," I added softly, just for him.

"I will. Good night, Flavie."

It took us but a few minutes to get back to the inn. After Romaric parked the car, I followed him into the house, while Gwenn went to quickly check on the horses. Or at least, that's what she said, but I caught a glimpse of her typing on her cell phone. Maybe the horses weren't the only ones she wanted to check on, I thought, as I noticed the dreamy smile that appeared on her lips.

Inside the B & B, I took off Romaric's jacket, although reluctantly, and gave it back to him. Deep down inside, a part of me hoped that my scent would linger in it, and make him think of me the next time he wore it.

Yes, I was aware that I should know better than to daydream like that about a man I had just met who was probably not interested in me, or at least not in a romantic way, but I was a romance novelist. Imagining romantic gestures and situations was in the job description—and I wasn't above fantasizing that my life was a romance novel from time to time.

"Thank you for lending it to me," I said softly, my eyes catching his.

He smiled, and once again, the ground seemed to move under my feet.

"You are welcome. Are you warm enough now? If not, please keep it."

"Thanks, I'm fine now."

Not that I would have minded keeping it, but it was better not to.

I might have worn it to bed and never taken it off again. Ever.

"As you wish," he said, flashing me another of his ground-shaking smiles. My blood ran quicker through my veins. Again.

Silence fell in the house, but we kept looking at each other, as if time itself had stopped.

"Well . . . good night," I said, finally.

"Good night."

That's when Gwenn came rushing into the inn, a huge smile on her lips, her phone still in her hands.

Well, apparently, "the horses" were really fine.

"Well, good night, Flavie, sleep tight!" she whispered, disappearing into their private quarters in the house. "See you tomorrow!"

"Yes, see you tomorrow, Gwenn! Good night, Romaric."

"Good night, Flavie."

And on those words, I climbed the stairs leading up to my room, feeling his eyes on me the whole time.

Chapter 10

I got up early the next morning, awoken after a too-short and dream-filled night by the loud thump of a boot falling on the floor and the whispering of obnoxious riders as they were getting ready in the room next to mine. Ten minutes later, I knew all about their plans for the day—apparently, there was a very nice creek a few hours' ride away that was perfect for a picnic. I had to admit that I wouldn't have minded joining them—and I had given up all hope of going back to sleep. After a quick shower, I went to sit in the sun on the terrace of the bed-and-breakfast with my knitting while I waited for the riders to leave and for breakfast to be served.

"That looks pretty," a voice behind me said. "Is it for a baby?"

I smiled as I turned my head. Romaric leaned against the door, the morning sun highlighting streaks of red in his dark hair. Images of my dreams rushed into my mind, and I did my best to act naturally, and not to blush.

"Actually, it's for a penguin," I answered innocently.

Romaric looked confused.

Amused, I told him more about the project. "It's for an Australian charity that tries to protect penguins that were caught in oil spills. If they're wearing sweaters, they can't try to clean themselves with their beaks and get oil poisoning. And the sweaters keep them warm, since the oil strips their natural protection away. My friends and I are knitting a few sweaters to contribute."

"Sweaters for penguins?"

"Yes, sir."

"You're sure this isn't a hoax?"

I got where he was coming from. I'd reacted pretty much the same way when Angélique had come up with the idea. But we'd looked it up and lo and behold, it really was a legitimate organization, so we'd charged ahead with our usual enthusiasm. It is kind of cool to think somewhere out in the world a cute little penguin will be wearing a sweater lovingly knitted by me.

"I am."

"Huh. You learn something new every day. I didn't think penguins needed sweaters."

"Only the ones caught in oil spills. Most get by just fine without them."

"I see. That's an important distinction."

"An essential one."

He smiled, amused.

This time, the world didn't shake, but I suspect it was only because my feet weren't on the ground.

His smile was bright enough to set a few hearts aflutter. Mine included.

"Breakfast's ready, if you'd like."

"Let me finish this row and I'll be right there."

"Any plans for today?" Romaric asked a little while later, pouring himself a steaming cup of coffee and leaning against the kitchen counter to sip it.

I swallowed a mouthful of the huge breakfast he'd prepared. Cereal, yogurt, toasted baguette, cheese omelet . . . I was going to need all day to work this off. I leaned back in my chair with my mug of tea, and peered at him over the rim.

"I was planning on visiting Kerzalec manor. I heard it was built in the fifteenth century by a local count, was seized after the Revolution, sold, and then bought again by another family. Is that all true?"

"Indeed it is. The manor was converted into a museum sometime during the twentieth century by the current owner, and it's amazing what he recovered to re-create the feeling of the seventeenth and eighteenth centuries. When you walk inside, it's as though time has stopped. It's quite a unique place in Brittany, and as a history teacher, you're bound to love it. And the park is beautiful during high summer. Did you know Erwan sculpted the fountain at the foot of the main building?"

My eyes widened in surprise. That *was* an interesting tidbit of knowledge! "I didn't! I can't miss it now."

"It's . . . pretty good. Actually, scratch that, it's beautiful."

"You're teasing me! Come on, tell me more. When did he sculpt it?"

Romaric smiled. "Maybe thirty years ago. In the early eighties, I think. I was too small to remember it properly, but Erwan's told me the story. Some man with a lot of money bought the place and restored it, made it almost as good as new. During the renovation, they found a few documents dating back to the nineteenth century, among which were plans for a stone fountain with a statue in the middle. The owner had heard of Erwan, of his work during his training as a stonemason. You know he is a Compagnon, right?"

There was pride in his voice. I nodded.

"So one day, the new owner of Kerzalec comes up to Erwan's workshop and says *Mr. Kermarrec, I've seen your work and you're very skilled. I'm restoring Kerzalec manor and I want you to be a part of my team. Are you in?*"

"Just like that?"

"Just like that."

"What did Erwan say?"

"*Let's see what you're offering.* The owner unfolded the plans for the fountain and showed them to Erwan."

"How did Erwan react?"

"He made up his mind on the spot. He looked at the owner and reached out to shake his hand. *When do I start?* he asked. And that was it. It took him almost a year to finish the fountain working alongside a hydraulics expert."

"I love that story! And now I'm even more eager to see the fountain. Do you know if there are any other examples of his work around here?"

"There are a few, yes," he answered with a smile. "Not all of them are available to the public. Some are part of private collections, but there are several that were commissioned by local councils. He's a peerless stonemason and an even better sculptor. He's a stonemason by trade, and that's how he makes a living, but his real passion is sculpture."

"I saw the Virgin Mary he gave to the church of Karouac. It's gorgeous. You'd swear she could breathe."

"I'd love to see that."

"I've got a picture of it in my room. I'll show it to you."

"That would be great, thanks. Can you believe that I'd never heard of Karouac, that statue, or anything that happened back then?"

"I think it's the same for everybody. For the life of me, I couldn't tell you what my father was like when he was twenty years old, what he thought, or what happened to him. I know a couple of things, but that's about it. It's like he sprung into being the way I know him right now. But he was a little boy first, and then a teenager who probably had a rebellious phase like anyone else..." As I was speaking the words, I realized they were true. What do we really know about another person's past?

"You never think about the members of your family having a life before you came into the picture. I don't think either Gwenn or I ever asked Erwan about his training and the journey he made across France. I've seen pictures of his final work, the one he presented for full Compagnon status, but I don't know anything about the people he met or the things he lived through during those years. It's kind of a shame, when you think about it."

"You know what they say. Never too late to start."

"You're right. But it is a shame that you had to come into our lives for us to start asking questions."

Embarrassed, I laughed and quickly changed the subject. "Tell me, is there a place I can find a list of Erwan's viewable artwork?"

"On his company's website. There's a page about his sculptures."

"There's a website?" I frowned, bemused. "How come I didn't find it when I tried to look him up?"

Romaric frowned. "I don't know. You should have. I know updating it isn't Erwan's priority, but you should have been able to find it. It could be the referencing isn't good enough. I'll look into it. I keep telling Erwan he could create more opportunities if he consistently updated it and posted more articles. He always says he has more than enough orders and that in his line of work, the best publicity is by word of mouth. And since he'll be retiring this year, I guess he's not interested in making the effort."

"I guess I see his point. Still, can you give me the web address?"

"Sure."

He wrote it down on a sticky note, which he handed over. I thanked him and gazed at it for a few moments. Taille de Pierre, Pierre de Taille. What a lovely name for a company! It was a sort of pun: *Taille de pierre* is the act of shaping the stone and *pierre de taille* is the material, the stone used for carving, and the name for a standard block of stone used in stone building. The name couldn't have been better chosen. I thought it fit Erwan to a T.

"Thank you very much. I'll look into it as soon as possible."

I laid the note by my breakfast plate and stared at it, sipping my tea.

Another hidden part of Erwan's life was unfolding before me, and I couldn't wait to discover his sculptures.

I wanted to find out everything there was to know about him.

Over the course of a single evening, he had become very important to me. I was used to thinking of my father as my only family, and it was strange to feel so close to someone I had met so recently, even though it somehow felt as though I had known him for much longer . . .

"You're so lucky to have him."

"I know. He's a wonderful person."

"He is," I replied.

"When our parents died twenty years ago, he was the one who took us in. He fought to get custody of us and he raised me and my sister. He was father and mother both, and he was an extraordinary parent—considerate, thoughtful. We owe him everything we are today. After our parents died . . . let's just say we were two young and difficult kids, but he gave us all the love, the attention, and the space we needed. He let us grieve and have our own space. Then one day he took us to our parents' grave and told us dozens of little stories about them.

"Things got better after that. We still missed our parents, but we'd learned to accept that they were gone and move on with our lives, and it was all thanks to him. I think if I only had to remember one thing about him, it would be his dedication to raising us. He's still very much a part of our lives today. He's our anchor, for both of us."

"I'm so sorry about your parents," I murmured.

"Thanks. If Erwan hadn't been there, we wouldn't be the people we are today."

"He's very important to you."

"More than anyone else in the world."

"I understand. I feel the same about my father."

There was a moment's silence before Romaric broke it. "I don't know exactly what happened with the woman in the letter, but—"

"Amélie."

"Amélie, right. I can't help thinking that if she never tried to find him again, maybe she didn't deserve him. Maybe she didn't feel for Erwan the same way he did for her."

"Perhaps it's more complicated than we think. Remember, she never got his letter."

"But she never tried to write or call," he pointed out.

"Not that we know of, but we haven't heard her side of the story. We don't know what really happened to her. Maybe she fell ill. Maybe she tried to find him, and they missed each other. Or she didn't know where to find him. Maybe their entire lives are peppered with missed encounters."

"She could have gone to the Compagnons to find out where he was; they probably knew."

"Maybe she did and they wouldn't tell her. The woman in charge of the Brest boarding house didn't want to release the information to me," I reminded him.

"But she called Erwan on your behalf. They probably would have done the same for Amélie if she'd tried."

He had a point.

"I can't help thinking she just wanted to have a bit of fun, and when he left, she ended up marrying someone else."

"But that happened several years later. And she divorced him afterwards. I know the sixties weren't that far back, with all the unrest and social revolution in France, and women taking actions to emancipate themselves from the yoke of society, but we have to remember that the communication we take for granted today wasn't available then. I have a feeling that Amélie was a very caring person."

"How do you know? Have you spoken to her?"

"No. It's just that since I found the letter, I've learned a lot about her. And my impressions don't fit with the person you think she is, that's all."

He sighed, and I wondered what he was thinking. I hoped I hadn't upset him, that my theories or my defending Amélie hadn't offended him. I could understand why he was so unwilling to trust her. He loved Erwan like a father, and Erwan had suffered because of Amélie. It was only natural Romaric should want to protect him.

But I couldn't just sit by and listen. Not after what I had learned, after what Erwan had told me yesterday. I was convinced that in this particular case, blame could be shared. It had taken two to tango. But

I was reasonably certain that their story of lost love had more to do with timing, circumstances, and of course, age. They were so young at the time.

I knew, however, that there would be no convincing Romaric. That was one conversation he would have to have with Erwan, not me.

In any case, I didn't hold all the pieces to the puzzle. How could I argue my case when I was missing crucial evidence? I needed to wait and find out more.

"It's in the past, anyway," Romaric reasoned. "Let's leave it there. It's for the best. So," he went on, evidently eager to change the subject, "what will you do now that you have solved the mystery of the waylaid letter? Any other history projects?"

"Well, for now my only plans are to enjoy my holiday here."

"Excellent idea. You have my seal of approval."

Once again, he smiled at me, and the effect was the same. My heart fluttered. My stomach too. Heaven help me, the man was breathtaking.

"What about after that? When you return to Karouac?"

"My father's birthday is the day after I get back, and then I promised him I'd help him inventory his shop."

"What kind of shop does he have?"

"An antiques shop."

"So no more digging up dusty archives?"

I hesitated, then decided to be completely honest with him. "Actually, I do have some plans regarding Erwan's letter."

Romaric frowned. Poor guy, he'd thought I was done and moving on . . .

"What are they?"

"Well"—I grimaced an apology—"I'm going to turn Erwan's story into a novel . . ."

A few dozen kilometers away, Erwan was teaching one of his monthly classes—or at least trying to. He couldn't focus on the young *aspirants* he was instructing.

Last night's conversation with Flavie kept intruding, going through his mind over and over again, leaving him unable to think of anything else.

Fight. Fight for Amélie and win her back.

Forty-five years had gone by. Wasn't it too late by now?

She'd probably forgotten him.

But he couldn't resist the urge to see her, speak to her, try to explain, try to understand. Try to make her understand.

He'd tried so hard to move past her. He'd tried to forget her for decades in an effort not to suffer as much as he had during those first years, and all of that had come to nothing when Flavie told him about the letter. The pain had bloomed as fast and as powerfully as it had on the first day. Worse, even, because now he had to wonder if he hadn't made a mistake. If everything had been his fault after all.

But he couldn't blame Flavie for bringing the truth to light, even though it shattered the peace he'd built so painstakingly.

He blamed himself.

He remembered what Father François had told him on the day he'd left Karouac: *If she's meant to be with you, you won't lose her. The Lord will reunite you, whatever may happen.*

Suddenly a terrifying thought crossed his mind. What if it was happening again?

What if he was letting his chance slip away forever, for fear of what might happen when they came face-to-face?

Erwan had never been a believer, but today he was ready to make some concessions.

Maybe Father François had been right. Maybe the Lord did have a plan for them—and He was bringing them back together.

Chapter 11

Romaric had been telling the truth. The fountain was gorgeous. It had a round pool about three meters across, and the statue at the center was of a young woman pouring water out of a long, thin jar sitting on her left shoulder. She was looking down, as though considering something at her feet, a half smile playing on her lips. She was naked from the waist up, a drapery wrapped around her hips.

I sat on the bench across from the fountain and gazed at her face for a long time, letting my thoughts wander.

Erwan, Romaric, Amélie, Gwenn, the penguins, Liam and Clarissa, Erwan and Amélie again . . . A thousand questions went through my head. Was I right to come here? Should I try to reunite Erwan and Amélie? Was Romaric attracted to me? The thought drifted through my mind, and stopped me short. Ever since last night, I hadn't been able to stop thinking about him. But it had to stop. I had to stop. I was here, in the beautiful little town of Port-l'Abbé, to return Erwan's lost letter to him—not to look for romance. Well, in a way it was a mission that was about romance, but not mine. It was for Erwan and Amélie. I had to make sure I wasn't sidetracked by Erwan's gorgeous nephew.

Well, any more than I had already been, in any case.

Dismissing (or at least, trying to) thoughts of Romaric, I returned to the questions that were popping up. I did want to go riding, but could I get back in the saddle without looking ridiculous? It had been quite a long time since I'd had riding lessons.

Finally, my thoughts came back to my current work. Was I going to finish writing Liam and Clarissa's story, or were they going to stay parked in a corner of my head gathering dust, the way they had over the last few weeks? I would have to get back to them someday soon, whether I wanted to or not. My publisher was waiting for them—and for me.

I examined the statue's face carefully, as though the answers might be in the fold of her eyelids, the curve of her lips, the gentle slope of her chin, or the pure lines of her high cheekbones. The longer I looked at her, the more her face seemed familiar to me. On a hunch, I opened my purse and took out the article about Erwan's Virgin Mary I'd brought along.

My memory had not been deceiving me. The faces of both statues were nearly identical. My imagination immediately went into overdrive. Could it be . . . Amélie's face? If only I had a picture of her! I longed to find out if my theory was true.

Another idea flashed through my mind. What if Erwan had carved the same face on all the statues of women he sculpted? Assuming he sculpted other women, of course. There was only one way to find out. I dug my phone out of my pocket and opened the browser app. I typed in the address to Erwan's website, cursing against the poor network connection when the page loaded at a snail's pace.

Of course, when it finally did upload, I could see only half the website—it hadn't been designed with phone access in mind. But I only cared about the photos. I clicked on the gallery of pictures and scrolled through Erwan's work. An arched vault, several chimneys, a few façades . . . There! Another statue of a woman! Same face. I rapidly found a third, then a fourth, and a fifth dating back ten years. Each was different . . . but they all shared the same face.

It had to be Amélie's face.

I closed the browser page and searched through my phone book for Chantale's number.

I had a few questions for her.

"Flaviiiie! Cécile here!"

I had been savoring the final bites of my dessert on the beach, digging my toes into the sand and admiring the sunset setting the sky ablaze when my phone rang.

On a whim, I had decided to have a picnic on the beach and bring my knitting along. I'd bought a salad, a bottle of peach iced tea and an almond tartlet—two, actually, because they only sold them in pairs—at the local grocery store. I'd also made a side trip to a small antiques shop where I'd found several valuable rare coins that my father, ever the coin collector, would love.

I'd slipped back into the bed-and-breakfast to drop off my purchases and gone down to the beach, settling near a small cove out of the wind and away from the few tourists stubbornly going for a swim. My evening alone with my knitting had seemed like the perfect moment to reflect on what I had learned.

"Hey, Cess. What's up?" I asked as I lowered my bottle of iced tea into the sand. I had emailed the girls when I got back to the bed-and-breakfast earlier, bringing them up-to-date about Amélie's face, Gwenn's humor, Erwan's kindness . . . and Romaric's smile.

"Oh, nothing much. I'm with all the girls. We decided to hold an impromptu meeting at Bérénice's shop so you could tell us everything! Your email was waaaay too short. Everybody agrees with me. Are we interrupting something?"

"Nope. I'm on the beach, enjoying the sunset. It's beautiful, by the way."

"Okay, we're all here, you're on speaker. Say hi to everyone!"

"Hi, everyone!"

A jumble of noise came over the line. I could make out some of it: "Hey!" "Hi, Flavie!" "Tell us about Romaric!" "Is he really a hottie?" "Why do you always get the cuties? I'm so jealous!"

"Wait a minute. I told you that Erwan is still madly in love with Amélie, and the only thing you remember from my email is that Romaric is even better looking than his uncle was when he was twenty?"

"Was there any other interpretation of that email?" Angélique asked sweetly, as though butter wouldn't melt in her mouth. "Flavie, Erwan is obviously in love with Amélie—that's not news, and anyway, he's too old for you. What we want to know is whether you've got a chance with the hot nephew. You deserve to have a bit of fun . . ."

I sighed. "You all are insufferable."

"We know you love us. Come on, spill. What's he like?"

I closed my eyes and pictured Romaric, something that I had been doing quite often for the last twenty-four hours: his mesmerizing gaze, so deep and intense it made me dizzy, his lean, muscled build that was somehow so comforting, his smile that made me want to smile back at him forever. I thought about the strange and unexpected feeling of warmth and welcome I'd experienced when he'd shrugged out of his jacket and laid it over my shoulders last night, about his quick and easy sense of humor. About everything that was him.

He was attractive. *Very* attractive. Maybe even *too* attractive. It had been a long time since I'd been so taken with someone, especially someone I'd only just met. The pull I felt was physical, almost magnetic, and stirred deep sensual instincts within me. In a way, it was nice to feel alive, thrumming with desire, but it was also disconcerting. I hadn't been prepared for that. And I wasn't sure what would come of it. Heartbreak, maybe.

Lucky for me, years of teaching experience had taught me to be cool and collected no matter the circumstances, and I made the most of it. I wasn't sure I was ready to admit out loud how much I was attracted to him.

"He's . . ." I hesitated, then changed tracks. "Let's just say he looks like Superman and acts like that guy in *Pacific Rim*. You know, the hero, I can never remember his name."

"Charlie Hunnam?"

"Yeah, him. Or his character, anyway. You know, smiling, charming, protective, kind, and he has a great sense of humor."

"You mean the kind of man you only find in books," Angélique said rhetorically.

"Yeah, more or less."

"I repeat," Bérénice interjected, "I am jealous as hell."

"And the most important question," Vic said, cutting in. "Do you like him?"

"I don't think there is a single woman on Earth who would not like him."

"You're not answering the question, Flavie," Vic reminded me.

I grimaced. They knew me too well. "I met him yesterday, Vic. It's too early to tell if I truly like him."

"So what you're carefully *not* saying is that you're really into him."

"All right, you win! I think he's cute as hell and absolutely irresistible. Happy now?"

"Only if you know what you have to do next . . ."

"What?"

"Go for it!"

Easier said than done. Even if a part of me really, really wanted to. "Okay, moving on. You want to know what Chantale told me?"

"She called you back after talking to her sister?" I could hear the excitement in Vic's voice.

I had asked Chantale about the reason for Amélie's divorce when I called her this morning, explaining honestly why I was asking. Excited about my theory and the fact that Erwan was still very much in love with her, she had immediately called her sister to dig into the past and ask a few questions on my behalf, and called me back a few hours later—actually, as I was grocery shopping for my picnic.

"Yup. That she did."

"We're all ears."

"According to Chantale's sister, France, things didn't work out so well with Amélie's husband, which is why they got divorced. And France thinks the reason they never worked out, though Amélie never admitted it, is that she never forgot about Erwan, try as she might."

"What are you going to do about it?" Bérénice asked.

"Nothing just yet. I don't want to rush anything and I certainly don't want to bully Erwan into something he's not ready for. But I offered to give him Amélie's phone number and address yesterday."

"You did?" Bérénice asked.

In the background, I could hear someone saying, "He isn't ready? For goodness sake, it's been forty-five years!" I didn't ask who had made the comment. Instead, I responded to Bérénice.

"Uh-huh. I don't think Romaric would like that very much if he knew, by the way. He thinks the past should stay in the past."

"Well, he does have a point," Vic argued, pragmatic as always.

"I know. Which is why I'm not going to push. But if Erwan asks me, I'm not going to lie. I'll tell him what I know."

"What if Romaric resents that?"

I looked down, hoping with all my might that it wouldn't come to that, but knowing that if Erwan did accept my offer, Romaric probably wouldn't be enthusiastic. I didn't like the idea of doing this behind his back—though technically, he was there the first time I'd offered to give his uncle Amélie's number . . .

But what he didn't know was that I'd brought the topic up again with Erwan later that evening, and frankly, after Romaric told me how he felt about Amélie this morning, I didn't want to speak of it again. I was afraid our tentative connection would fizzle out as quickly as it had bloomed.

And I would really hate that.

"He'll have to deal with it," I replied in the end. I didn't know what else to say. "It's Erwan's decision, not his. It's not even mine. But we still have a way to go before hitting that roadblock, if we ever come to it. For now, I'm just going to enjoy my time here and try to do some groundwork for what comes next. Because brace yourselves, girls—I haven't told you yet, but Erwan is okay with me writing a novel inspired by his story . . ."

There was an explosion of reactions over the line.

"That is sooooo cool!"

"I just know that with you writing it, that story is going to be fantastic!"

"Speaking of which," Cess chimed in, "when you get back we have to get together and open our predictions to find out who won the bet!"

"I look forward to it. But I can pretty much tell you already that I was way off base. I can't wait to find out what you all wrote."

"It's a date then. See you when you get home!"

Movement at the corner of my eye caught my attention. A horse and rider were coming my way, silhouetted against the horizon. The last rays of sunlight cast a warm glow on the man's brown hair and the horse's glossy gray-black coat.

My heart skipped a beat when I recognized the rider.

Romaric.

He must have seen me, because he veered off his path to come straight to me.

"I have to go," I said in a rush. "I'll call you back when I know more."

"What? What's happening?" Vic asked.

"I'll tell you later. Bye!" I hung up just as Romaric rode up to me.

"Hi," he called, swinging down from the saddle and smiling at me.

"Hi." I tried to seem unruffled and not at all as if his smile made me turn to butter.

"How was your day?"

I could tell from the way he looked at me that he wasn't just asking out of politeness. He was sincerely interested, and I couldn't help but feel flattered.

It was silly to react that way to such a small thing, but what can you do? I wasn't quite myself whenever he was around, that much was clear.

And it got worse with every meeting. He was making my heart pound. The man's effect on me was potent. "Great, thanks." I tried to look smooth and unconcerned. "What about you?"

"In the Kermarrec family, a day spent in the saddle is always a good day," he replied.

"Did you go riding with the group, or were you on your own?" I asked.

"They left this morning and Gwenn had to go to Brest, so yes, I was on my own."

"You should have told me. I'd have asked you to come sightseeing with me."

I thought about how lovely it would have been to have him along as I explored the manor. Something, a sixth sense perhaps—or maybe the fact that he and his uncle had spent part of the previous evening narrating various local legends, to my great delight—told me that he would have been much better company than the freshman college student who had been in charge of the guided tour. He'd seemed about as interested in his surroundings as I was in the periodic table.

"That's all right." Romaric shrugged. "I had things to do here anyway. What did you think of Kerzalec?"

"It was wonderful. You were right about the statue, too—a real masterpiece. I think I spent an hour looking at it."

For a minute, I thought of telling him about Karouac's Virgin Mary statue and the other masterpieces Erwan had carved, and Amélie's face, but I managed to bite my tongue. Even though I would have liked to share my findings and tell him about my conversation with Chantale, I didn't want us to argue about Amélie. Not tonight at least. I was enjoying the way he was looking at me, and the warmth in his gaze held me captive.

The big revelation could wait a bit longer.

And besides, he might already have noticed the similarity of the faces on Erwan's statues.

"I told you." Romaric seemed to swell with pride. "Erwan is the best sculptor in Brittany. Maybe even the best in France."

"Whoa, hold your horses. Or horse, as it may be," I teased. "But you're right, he is very skilled." I smiled as I reached out and stroked his horse's nose. "Your horse is gorgeous."

"Flavie, this is Moonlight. Moonlight, meet Flavie."

"Hi, Moonlight. We haven't met before, but I've been admiring you from afar ever since I got here . . . You *are* gorgeous, you know," I repeated.

He sniffed at my hand and neighed softly.

"That means he thinks you smell good."

"Why, thanks!" I quipped, amused. "You're a real gentleman," I added, addressing Moonlight.

"He is. For example, he's really protective with Belle."

"Is that the white mare I saw across the pen?"

"That's her. She belongs to Gwenn."

"Is she your girlfriend? Your one true love?" I asked the horse.

He bobbed his head as though he understood and agreed. Either the horse was psychic, or I saw answers where there were only coincidences. Still, at least I was having a lot of fun.

"You'll have to introduce me, then," I told Moonlight.

"You can meet her when I take you for a ride," Romaric replied for him. "Maybe the day after tomorrow, on the fourteenth? We could go for a ride and come back in time for the party and fireworks. If you have a date to dance with Erwan, you can't miss that."

"Certainly not. But you're sure Gwenn won't mind? I don't want to take her horse away."

"Don't worry, she's perfectly fine with it."

"Then I'd love to."

Romaric's face lit up. "Great! I'll set it up tomorrow. I know the perfect place, and I think you're going to love it."

"Where will you be taking me?"

"It's a surprise. Trust me, you'll like it."

"All right. I leave the planning in your capable hands."

"Still working on your baby-seal sweaters?" He gestured at the abandoned knitting on my picnic blanket.

"*Penguin* sweaters. I'm almost done."

"I'll leave you to it, then. I'd hate to be responsible for leaving the penguins in the cold . . ."

"Would you . . . Would you like to join me?" I offered timidly. "I have some tea left, though it's barely iced anymore, and I have an extra almond tartlet, if you'd like that."

His gaze met mine, and my heart skipped a beat.

"I would enjoy it very much. But I don't want to intrude."

"You wouldn't be. Not at all. I mean—" I stopped, unable to recall what I had meant to say. Chances were it probably wasn't that important, anyway. My brain cells seemed to have fled, leaving me stammering like a teenager.

Thank God I was usually smoother than this. Otherwise, my students probably would make short work of me.

"All right," he said. "I'm in." He smiled again, and once more, I felt the earth shake beneath my feet.

Chapter 12

"**R**eady to go for a ride?" Romaric asked when I joined him in the stables two days later.

The previous day had been fun, a real holiday lazing about and taking long walks on the beach. Upon returning to the inn, I'd caught a glimpse of Romaric brushing the horses—shirtless. I admit I got carried away fantasizing about his perfect body for a moment or two, right up until Gwenn came up to ask me if I had a little time to spare to teach her how to knit.

When she found me drooling over her brother, she abandoned for a minute all thought of learning to knit. She was much more interested in playing matchmaker. After a fruitless attempt to convince her that no, I was not in the market for romance—which was, strictly speaking, the truth—I'd simply given up and changed the subject. She'd been kind enough not to bring it up again.

We'd spent the rest of the day together knitting sweaters for penguins—or at least, I was knitting and she was watching me and learning the ropes—and chatting away about various topics such as our jobs, the horses, the bed-and-breakfast, tourists, tides, men, Port-l'Abbé, Karouac, Erwan, Amélie . . . and most definitely not mentioning Romaric. I'd told her about wanting to write the story of Amélie and Erwan, and she'd asked to read it once I was done. I said yes, of course, and I wondered what it would feel like to read the story of someone you were so close to. I verbalized this, and we discussed it for a long time before the conversation circled back to my search for Erwan . . . and Amélie. When Gwenn asked me about her, I told her everything I knew. Her opinion on her uncle's long-lost love, I quickly realized, was more nuanced than Romaric's. She, like me, was curious to know what exactly had happened and if there was a way to fix it. Little by little, we'd come to speak of lost moments, and life in general. And somehow, in the midst of our conversation, we slipped into what resembled friendship.

That day, I discovered that Gwenn, like her uncle and brother, was both considerate and kind. The rush of affection I had felt for her when we'd met had proved to be justified. She had charmed me just the way Erwan had. Her brother charmed me in other ways—and I still didn't know exactly how that came to happen or what would come of it.

We'd ended the day by having dinner at Erwan's with the entire family, and once more, the ground under my feet had shaken so hard I had been afraid it would give way.

I had gone to sleep utterly won over by this family that I was growing fonder of by the minute. Which, of course, was not going to make leaving any easier as my time with them ticked away.

After such delightful days, I was starting to dread returning to my everyday routine. I knew I was going to miss Erwan, Romaric, and Gwenn something awful when I returned to Karouac.

But for now, I'm still here, I thought, catching Romaric's eye as he waited to lead me on what promised to be a memorable ride.

"Ready and raring to go!" I exclaimed, lifting my arms and twirling around.

"That you are," he said, looking me up and down appreciatively. "Seems like you found everything you needed in Gwenn's wardrobe."

I glanced down. I had mentioned to Gwenn the day before that I didn't have anything appropriate for riding, and she'd immediately offered to lend me an outfit. I was slightly shorter and slimmer than she was, but she'd chosen something that was "a bit snug" for her. I was wearing gray and black riding breeches with high black leather riding boots—luckily enough, we had the same shoe size—and a black cotton halter top. The finishing touch was the black riding helmet, something Gwenn had told me I could not do without.

I'd taken a long look in the mirror before coming down to join Romaric, and I had to say the effect was kind of spectacular. I felt like a female Indiana Jones, utterly confident and sexy, ready to face any adventures that fate—and Romaric—would send my way. Excitement bubbled inside me. Searching for Erwan and Amélie had been the wildest thing I'd done since . . . since I'd become a teacher, really. But today, I was anything but the professor, and I was determined that for once, I, rather than characters in my book, would live the adventures.

I looked up and shot Romaric a smile that fit my mood—daring. "It was really sweet of her to offer. I didn't have anything appropriate and I doubt a dress would have been very convenient."

"It suits you," he said, still staring at me.

"Thank you." I could feel the heat rising in my cheeks. "You're not too shabby yourself."

Understatement of the year. Or the century.

He was gorgeous.

His brown riding breeches hugged his muscles in a very flattering manner, and his white T-shirt made a stark contrast with his tanned skin and his blue eyes. Along with the black riding boots, it was a simple outfit, but he took it to a new level and made it look sexy as hell.

As if he weren't attractive enough.

"So what's the plan?" I asked, trying to look more relaxed than I actually was. "Unless that's a surprise too . . ."

His gaze snapped up to my face. "The destination is a surprise, not the journey," he said. "How about we start with an hour's lesson on the basics to ease you into the saddle. Remind me, have you ever ridden before?"

"A few hours a long time ago. Nothing really noteworthy."

"Okay, we'll take this from the top. Let me introduce you to your mount."

I followed him into the stables. Two heads were poking out from the ten-odd stalls inside. As if he recognized me, Moonlight stretched his neck to sniff at me.

"Hey, you," I murmured as I drew closer to stroke his nose.

He whinnied softly.

"He says he's glad to see you again," Romaric translated.

"So you do speak horse, then?" I teased, glancing at him from under my lashes.

"I took a course," he assured me with a straight face. "I was pretty good, but I had to drop it in high school since they didn't offer the class anymore."

My lips quirked, amused by his particular brand of humor.

"And this is Belle."

I stepped closer to finally meet the gorgeous white mare I'd only seen from afar up to now.

"Hi, Belle. Your name is perfect for you."

I stroked her forehead wordlessly for several moments, mesmerized by her grace and beauty. She was a princess among horses. She tolerated my attention with equanimity, even seeming to enjoy it. She nuzzled my hand, probably looking for something to eat. Gwenn had advised me to bring apples, so I fed her one and gave the other to Moonlight.

"Are you trying to bribe them with apples?" Romaric asked from behind me.

From *just* behind me. He was so close that I could feel the warmth of his breath on my neck. An involuntary shiver ran up my back.

"Absolutely! Maybe this way I can get through this day with a minimum of bruises on my backside and without embarrassing myself in front of you!"

"Belle is a real sweetheart, so you're not going to fall off. But should it happen, I promise not to laugh."

"I certainly hope so!"

"Ready to go?"

"Ready when you are."

After saddling the horses and leading them outside, he started by explaining the basics to me: how to understand a horse's signals, Belle's in particular, how to hold the reins and sit in the saddle so as to move with the horse, not against her. He explained how I should give commands to Belle, how I should move depending on the horse's gait. Old memories surfaced, and I slipped back into the few skills I'd managed to attain during my beginner classes all those years ago.

When it was time to try out the theory for real, Romaric laid his hand on my waist to help me into the saddle. Of course, I immediately blushed and my heartbeat rocketed up, as it usually did. I didn't know whether it was the feel of his hand on my waist, firm and gentle, the heat of his body so close to mine, his watchful gaze on my face, or maybe all three at once, but I needed all my restraint not to jump him then and there and have my wicked way with him right in the middle of the field.

Of course, I held back. That would have been disastrous. After more or less jumping into his uncle's arms right after arriving, Romaric would think I was crazy if I did the same to him. Really, I had more self-control than that.

At least I hoped so.

Because right then I was a hairsbreadth away from giving in to my baser instincts.

If he could feel the tangled knot of my emotions, Romaric gave no sign of it, guiding me through sitting in the saddle correctly with the same cool, relaxed manner he'd had up till now. But when I was situated properly, a few endless seconds later, his hand lingered on my waist and his eyes stayed glued to mine for longer than seemed strictly necessary.

I thought I was done for.

About an hour later, Romaric estimated I was ready to ride. I wasn't too sure about that, but I certainly was ready to follow him to the ends of the earth. He packed a picnic into Moonlight's saddlebags and checked my seat on Belle one last time before he led the way into the forest. Our goal, he explained, was a beautiful clearing by a small pond in the middle of the forest.

"You're going to love it. It's safe from the tourists and full of legends and stories of star-crossed love," he added with a smile.

Our horses walked side by side on the wide trail as Romaric started to tell the tragic tale of Lovers' Lake, as the place was known.

According to legend, the pond had been born of the tears of a woman whose lover had been killed by her husband. He'd returned from hunting and found them in a most compromising position in the clearing where they had agreed to meet. In a rage, her husband had drawn his sword and killed his rival on the spot. Grief-stricken, the woman had fallen across her lover's lifeless body and wept for him for days on end, her tears forming a lake that rose around her and drowned her, leaving both of their bodies to lie together for eternity at the bottom.

It was the kind of tragic love story that would have been right at home among the folklore of Brocéliande, the legendary forest of Merlin, Arthur, and the Knights of the Round Table, situated in Brittany, a bit east from here.

No need to say, I was fascinated.

As soon as he was finished, I asked Romaric whether he knew even more of these tales, after he'd told so many of them over the last few days.

"Enough for you not to be bored until we reach Lovers' Lake!"

Completely focused on our conversation, I had ceased to pay attention to our surroundings. I had eyes only for Romaric. All I was aware of was his presence by my side, his warm and gentle voice lulling my thoughts and feeding my personal addictions—history, stories, him . . .

It happened so fast I never saw it coming, nor understood what was going on until it was over. Without any forewarning, Belle whinnied and started to stomp and buck. I barely had time to grasp onto her mane in order not to fall head over heels and break something. I cried out in surprise and fright before I caught myself and tried not to scare Belle even more. But my own panic was real. Very real indeed! Belle reared up, almost unseating me, and backed away as though something on the trail had scared her.

Millions of images sped through my mind, and for the first time, I regretted having such an overactive imagination. I could picture myself being thrown to the ground, crushed by a panicked horse, paralyzed for life and disfigured for the rest of my days. I tried to regain control by tightening my grip on Belle's glossy mane and trying to hold on with my calves, desperately hoping my muscles would be enough to keep me in the saddle. My heart was beating fit to burst.

Fortunately, Romaric, gentleman *and* savior, reacted at once. He swung out of the saddle and made a grab for Belle's reins, raising his voice to ask, "Are you all right?"

"I'm okay," I replied shakily, though I wasn't sure I was.

He nodded and pulled on Belle's reins to bring her back down on four legs, speaking to her in a low, reassuring voice. In spite of my fright, I couldn't help but admire his gentleness and calm. My heart thudded in my ears as he held the reins with one hand and stroked Belle's nose with the other. After what seemed like an eternity, Belle seemed to settle down. She stopped stomping and I could feel her flanks rising and falling more slowly as her breathing calmed.

The whole thing couldn't have lasted more than a minute, two tops, but it felt as though it had been hours. I felt empty, my muscles frozen.

Romaric gazed up at me, worry in his eyes. "Are you sure you're all right? You don't look too steady to me."

"I am now." I let out a long, slow breath. "Thank you. You're my hero," I quipped, trying to release the tension.

"I'm so sorry," he replied, ignoring my efforts. "She's never like this. Something must have scared her."

"It's fine. No harm done, right? Just a few years shaved off my life." I laughed, putting on a brave front.

I didn't want him to think I was weak; I was determined not to seem fragile in front of him. I wanted him to think I was strong, a true adventurer.

That was who I was supposed to be that day, right? Indiana Jones and Lara Croft would never have lost their cool over such a small thing.

He smiled and offered his hand for me to get down. In spite of my efforts to keep my dignity and not seem affected by what had just happened, my traitorous body let me down. As soon as my feet hit the ground, my knees gave way and I almost sagged. I reflexively grabbed onto Romaric's broad shoulders, and his hands found my waist in a firm grip. Our gazes met, and when his blue eyes found mine, my heart rate went straight back up—and this time, it wasn't out of fear.

"Whoops. You say you're okay, but your body and eyes are not matching your words." He frowned, obviously concerned.

"Uh, I think I'm fine now. I swear," I added as my legs came back under control and I straightened.

This time, my muscles obeyed and I managed to stay upright, sparing myself further embarrassment. "See? No more weak knees!" I raised my eyebrows.

He let go slowly, ready to catch me if I were to wobble again.

It didn't happen, to my great relief.

Well . . . not quite. My legs felt stiff and tired. Riding was fun, but it was tough work too.

"Okay," he said, keeping his eyes on me. "I think we need a break anyway. Belle needs to calm down and so do you. It's almost noon," he added, glancing at this watch. "Why don't we go back to the clearing we passed a few minutes ago and have our picnic there? We can ride on to the pond later if you still want to go."

Chapter 13

"What do you think scared her?" I asked Romaric a little while later when he sat down next to me.

We'd retraced our path as he suggested, and he took care of our horses while I spread our picnic blanket next to the tiny stream curving around the edge of the clearing. It probably flowed into Lovers' Lake, I thought. I had arranged the food then, and with a quick glance over my shoulder to make sure Romaric wasn't watching, I'd dropped onto the blanket with about as much grace as a cow, my legs weak from riding and fright.

I may have played at being a supremely cool Lara Croft in front of Romaric, but inside, I had gotten a few years of my life scared out of me. I wasn't quite over it yet.

"I don't know," he replied, gazing at the horses.

Moonlight had drawn closer to Belle and it seemed as though he wanted to comfort her, rubbing his head against hers and up her neck, their manes mingling, neighing softly. Belle pressed closer to him as though his presence soothed her. I could almost see little hearts rising above them—they seemed to love each other as deeply as two people would.

Or maybe I was just fooling myself—entirely possible, but I liked my first interpretation better.

"A snake, maybe," Romaric went on, answering the question I had all but forgotten about. "But she'll be all right now."

"Moonlight will take care of her."

"In a way, yes."

"Can horses fall in love?" I wondered as I nibbled on a cherry tomato.

I could feel the adrenaline receding and my stomach making its presence known. I was ravenous. Some people say strong emotions make you hungry—it certainly had proven true for me at least.

Romaric shrugged. "Honestly, I'm not sure. Maybe. Why not? Horses can feel deep attachment to each other. That much is true, and sometimes to the extent that they suffer from being separated. I knew a stallion that pursued a mare and refused to breed with any other than his favorite. He'd follow her around and keep her away from other stallions. Is that love? I don't know. Maybe. It's hard to tell, they can't really communicate with us."

"Belle and Moonlight seem very fond of each other."

"They are. They've been living together for several years, and of course that creates a bond."

"Have you had them long?"

"We bought them when we opened the bed-and-breakfast ten years ago. We couldn't bear the thought of separating them, and anyway, we wanted a horse each. So we asked for a slightly larger loan than we'd planned on and bought both."

"How old are they?"

"Twelve."

"Is that old?" I asked him. I had no idea.

"Middle-aged. In human years, they'd be thirty-five to forty. In five or six years, we'll retire them."

"Oh. But you will keep them, won't you? Or will you sell them?" I asked anxiously.

"I don't think Gwenn has it in her to say goodbye to Belle, and I certainly couldn't send Moonlight away. They're part of our family now. I can't imagine selling them just because they got old."

"Phew! I was afraid they'd end up in an old-horse home . . ."

He laughed, and my heart practically stood still. "Not a chance. We love them way too much."

"Have you always been a horse rider?" I asked. I wanted to know all about him. It was strange. I'd never felt that way about any other man.

"As far back as I can remember. My parents loved horses and they'd go riding as often as they could. They taught us how to ride as soon as we could walk, or near enough. I wanted to be a horse vet when I was a kid."

"What changed your mind?"

"I don't precisely know. I grew up, realized I didn't really enjoy biology, so I thought about it, discussed it with Gwenn and Erwan, and I ended up going for a business degree. Then I opened the bed-and-breakfast with my sister."

"Do you ever regret not becoming a vet?"

"Never. I have horses in my life, and that's all I need. I enjoy my life the way it is. I like dealing with people, talking and exchanging ideas with them. I like knowing I can meet a range of individuals, from lawyers to sculptors, and they all share my love of horses. Once . . ."

I listened as he told me funny stories from his day-to-day life. I was curious, unable—unwilling, even—to resist the allure that attracted me to him.

It was too late anyway.

"But that's enough about me," Romaric concluded when he was done narrating one of his misfortunes in college. "Tell me about you."

"Me?" I said, startled. "There's really not much to say."

"Allow me to be the judge of that," he coaxed softly. "You're a teacher, a writer, a penguin-sweater knitter, a hobbyist detective . . ." He ticked off each point on a finger. "Where do you find the time to do all that?"

"I stole Hermione's Time-Turner," I claimed with a straight face.

"Don't say that. I might steal into your room tonight and make off with it. God knows I could use one!"

The thought of Romaric coming into my room in the middle of the night flashed through my mind, trailing a crowd of other, more sensuous images, and the butterflies in my stomach went wild.

"Seriously, what's your secret? Do you have a hidden identity? Is that it, are you actually Wonder Woman?"

I shrugged. "Nah, I'm just very organized. I almost never watch TV, I write instead early in the morning or during the evening. I take advantage of every minute in order to get everything done."

"And does everything get done?"

"Most of the time, yes. But it's easier when you don't have a husband or kids depending on you."

"There's no Mr. Richalet and no mini-you?"

"Nope."

Was that relief I had just seen flashing through his eyes, or did I simply want to think so? Unfortunately, the glint disappeared before I could decide.

His eyes stayed glued to mine for a few more seconds before he looked away and asked, "Are you really going to write Erwan's story?"

I sighed softly. I wished we could have talked about anything but that. I didn't want to cast a shadow on such a wonderful day. "Yes," I said honestly. "I really want to write it."

"Why?" he asked softly.

"Because it's beautiful, moving. Who wouldn't want to write that kind of story?"

"A tragic love story, you mean?" He raised his eyebrows, incredulous.

"No! That's not what I meant! It's not a tragic love story. It's a story that still isn't over, even forty-five years later. Their love transcends time and hurdles and it's still alive even when there's no hope left. How many people on earth do you think have known such love? How many were lucky enough to be loved the way Erwan loves Amélie? The way he still loves her today? How many?"

"I don't know, Flavie." His voice was barely a whisper. "I don't know. I'm not one of them."

"Me either," I confessed. "Which is why I need to write their story. Because it's magnificent and unique. Because I don't want it to be forgotten. Because . . . Because maybe this is my only chance to get close to something I might never get to experience other than by proxy."

I looked down, embarrassed I had poured out my feelings to him. I picked a daisy and started to pluck at its petals. I recalled the game I'd played so often as a child. *He loves me, he loves me not. He loves me, he loves me not . . .*

Slowly I plucked all the petals as the silence grew and grew. I could feel the weight of Romaric's gaze on me.

He loves me not.

I discarded the daisy and raised my eyes to his. I couldn't decipher what he was thinking. "You know," I said, "I promised Erwan that if he didn't feel up to reliving his history, I would let it go. I swear I'm not trying to make him suffer by reopening old wounds."

"I know, Flavie. I trust you."

"Oh. I thought you were going to tell me to drop it and leave the past where it belongs."

"I'm not going to lie to you. I've told you before and I haven't changed my mind, I'd rather the past stay in the past. Erwan lives a happy life and Amélie chose not to be a part of that life a long time ago."

I said nothing. I didn't quite agree with him—Erwan was happy, but clearly something was missing, a wound that had never healed. And I hardly thought Amélie had chosen to leave him behind.

But I kept my peace.

"However," Romaric continued, "I spoke with Erwan yesterday and I can tell he still loves her. And ever since you mentioned her, he's been itching to find her again."

"He said that?"

"Not as straightforwardly as that, no, but I can read between the lines. And I told him my opinion, but he's a grown man, he's allowed to make his own decisions. I'll support him whatever he chooses, and so will Gwenn."

I couldn't hold back my smile of relief. Romaric might be stubborn—a true Breton at heart!—but he was far from being narrow-minded or stupid. He knew what he had to do, and what Erwan needed.

"But frankly, if he does decide to drop this search, it'll be a relief. Because there's always a chance she won't want to see him, and I don't think he'd get over it this time."

"I agree."

Silence fell again, but our gazes stayed on each other, the air around us suddenly lighter. We had hashed it out, and now nothing could overshadow the faint inkling of something I felt stirring between us. The faint inkling of something I *wanted* to stir between us.

"Why don't we set that aside for now?" he offered, his eyes never leaving mine.

"Phew, yes, I was about to say as much. It's too beautiful a day to think of such serious matters. Hey," I improvised, grabbing at the first topic in my mind to change the subject, "has Belle ever had foals with Moonlight?"

And just like that, we were friends again and we went back to chatting about all kinds of things.

Romaric told me at length about his projects for the bed-and-breakfast, Belle and Moonlight. Business was good and he and Gwenn wanted to buy a couple more horses to offer rides to patrons who came horseless, as I had. I listened without interrupting, suggesting a few things here and there. Somewhere between the cheese and the brownie, I started telling him about my father and his shop. I skipped over my mother leaving when Romaric asked me why I never spoke of her. I didn't want another dark cloud on the remainder of our picnic.

Once the meal was over, a comfortable silence fell between us. I could feel drowsiness creeping up on me. I decided to copy Romaric and lie down on the blanket. Sunlight pierced through the treetops and leaves rustled in the wind, echoed by the gentle gurgle of the stream. Birds were singing, our horses were neighing softly across the clearing, and my eyelids were growing heavier and heavier. *Two minutes*, I thought to myself. *Less. Thirty seconds. I'll rest my eyes for thirty seconds.*

A raven's call startled me awake sometime later. I sprang up, my heart beating wildly, and looked around, trying to remember where I was. Romaric's gaze met mine, a smile upon his lips, and suddenly I recalled Belle spooking, the picnic and . . . Oh. I had fallen asleep. *Blast.*

Embarrassed, I apologized. "I'm really sorry. I didn't intend on falling asleep. This is so embarrassing."

"No need to apologize. Did you have a good nap, at least?"

"Yes, I suppose I really needed it. How long was I asleep? What time is it?"

"Nearly half past two."

"That late? I'm really, really sorry. I hope I didn't make you late for anything!"

"Don't worry." He waved a hand. "I set this afternoon aside for our ride, so no pressure." He hesitated, a glint of mischief in his eyes. "Are you aware that you talk in your sleep?"

Whoops! "What did I say?" I couldn't help but grimace. I *really* hoped I didn't moan his name . . .

"Nothing too compromising. I couldn't make anything out. You just . . . Well . . . It's nothing."

"Tell me!"

"Well, you mumbled a few words I didn't quite catch and . . . sighed a bit. Nothing really embarrassing or too coarse, just . . . you know. Kind of blissful."

I was ready to crawl into the ground. Any kind of hole, squirrel or mole, would have done the job. Instead, I did the only thing I could think of.

I hid my face in my hands. "God, please kill me now. I'm so sorry."

"Don't be. It was . . . adorable, actually."

"I don't think I'll ever get over it," I admitted, too flustered to dare look up into his face.

"I promise to take the secret to my grave."

"Thanks, that makes me feel so much better," I quipped, still slightly embarrassed.

At least I hadn't said anything compromising . . . That was something, wasn't it?

I looked around for a change of subject, eager to move on to something else, when I realized he was whittling a piece of wood. I couldn't see what form he was carving from where I sat.

I seized the opportunity like a lifeline. "You're an artist too?" I gestured to his hands.

"It's a hobby. Erwan taught me and I've been doing it for a long time. But unlike him, I only work with wood and I only do little pieces."

"Can I see?"

"Sure!"

He handed me the chunk of wood, and I could immediately tell what it was. "A bear cub!" I exclaimed, cradling it in my hands. "How cute!"

"Thank you," he replied modestly. "It's not quite done yet."

"It looks pretty much finished to me!"

"I still need to work on the rear legs and whittle down that knot on its neck, here and here," he explained, tracing the wood with his fingers to show me the improvements he wanted to add.

It had to happen sooner or later. It was pretty much inevitable.

As his fingers roamed over the wood, his hand brushed mine, and this simple touch made me shiver, just like it had a few nights ago. His hand lingered on the wooden bear, a hairsbreadth away from mine, our gazes crossed, and my thoughts scattered wildly.

"You, uh, y-you often carve wooden bears?" I stuttered, wrenching my eyes away.

"Often enough." His face was carefully composed as he moved his hand away, keeping his eyes on me. "I sell them in the Port-l'Abbé gift shop for a cheap price, just enough to buy the materials. It's a hobby, not a business."

I nodded, not quite sure what I was agreeing with. I examined the bear for a few more moments, long enough for my heart to settle down, then handed it back to him.

"I love it. It's really cute."

"Thank you." His hand brushed mine again as his fingers closed around the wood.

I knew he had done it on purpose this time. There was no other explanation. He wanted our hands to touch.

Why? I didn't dare hope he was as attracted to me as I was to him.

His eyes lingered on me for a few moments, then, wordlessly, he packed his equipment back into his saddlebags and rose, a tiny smile flickering on his lips.

"Ready to go on?"

Chapter 14

I spent a long time preparing to meet Romaric downstairs for the firemen's ball later that evening. I brushed my hair carefully, applied makeup just as carefully, then stood before the full-length mirror, holding two of my more stylish dresses in one hand, trying to decide which I should wear. I almost regretted not bringing my red dress, the one I'd bought for Angélique's wedding a few summers ago. It was plain enough, but with the right kind of jewelry you could spruce it up from business casual to wedding finery. The only issue was that it was a pain in the neck to wash, which meant I rarely took it out, even though I loved it. I hadn't even thought of packing it when I'd pulled out clothes for this short trip.

Who would have thought that I'd meet an irresistible, attractive, and funny man, one who would take me dancing at the July Fourteenth party? I certainly hadn't. I had expected to find Erwan, but not Romaric or Gwenn, or the feeling that I was perfectly at home with them.

I held the dresses in front of me, unable to decide which one would make me look more chic. *This evening I will be the prettiest woman at the dance . . .*

Or maybe not. There would probably be dozens of women wanting to dance with my partner, and some of them would certainly be prettier than me.

I gazed into the mirror, trying to be unbiased. I cleaned up well; I probably qualified as pretty, maybe even more than that, I hoped. My makeup emphasized my blue eyes, and I had gathered my hair in a loose bun at the nape of my neck with a few flyaway strands. I'd put on some gloss, a little blush, and a dab of perfume behind my ears. The only thing left was to choose a dress. Pink or blue? Blue or pink?

In the end, I went with the blue one, because it was the same shade as Romaric's eyes. As good a reason as any to make the choice, I guess.

I slipped it on, gave myself a last check—smoothing the front and back, double-checking my makeup—and stepped into the only pair of high-heeled sandals I'd brought on the trip, before closing the door behind me. Romaric was waiting at the bottom of the stairs, his back to me, breathtakingly elegant in cream-colored linen pants and a sky-blue shirt. Lucky coincidence—we'd match! The sound of my heels on the wooden stairs made him turn around and, for the thousandth time at least that day, my stomach started Zumba dancing.

"You're beautiful."

"You're not too bad yourself," I teased. At least I hoped it sounded teasing. I had never been very good at flirting; I found writing about it much easier than doing it myself.

Then Romaric did something so romantic that I literally stopped breathing for a few seconds. He lifted my hand, and kissed the top of it . . . a feathery, light touch. I had never had my hand kissed before. "Milady," he said softly, his eyes gazing into mine. "My humble self is at your service."

I muzzled my imagination before it could run wild and start suggesting what such a tender kiss could mean. I hardly knew what was happening to me these days. Usually my inspiration sparks fictional characters, but ever since I'd met Romaric's sky-blue eyes for the first time, my body had seemed to be drawn to him despite my best efforts. He played a starring role in my thoughts, or at least every spare thought that Amélie and Erwan weren't already a part of. I hadn't written a single word of my novel since I'd arrived here, but I had filled dozens of pages about Erwan and many more about his handsome nephew.

I hadn't dared read over what I had written, too afraid to find evidence that I was head over high heels for him.

"Are you ready, milady?" the subject of my thoughts asked, offering me his arm.

"I am ready, milord," I declared, slipping my arm through his.

"Here we go."

Erwan and Gwenn were already sitting at a table when we arrived at the ball. We slipped in next to them, and Romaric offered to get us drinks.

"Beer for me," Erwan said.

"Sex on the Beach cocktail," Gwenn replied.

Romaric raised an eyebrow. "It's a folk ball, Gwenn, not a nightclub. I'm pretty sure they don't have anything stronger than beer."

"Ask anyway. And if they don't have any, get me a juice."

Romaric turned to me.

"Same for me," I said.

"Sex on the Beach?" he asked with a devious half smile and a glint in his eyes.

A mix of mischief and something else I was too afraid to decipher.

It couldn't be . . . No, it couldn't be what I thought it was. I was probably misreading things again.

"No, uh, juice please," I stammered.

His smile widened—and he got to his feet. "Duly noted. I'll be right back."

He moved away, and my gaze followed him. He had a graceful, slightly feline stride—he probably was a very good dancer. He'd already proven he was a very good rider . . . and a very good sculptor . . . and—

"You're going to burn a hole in his shirt if you keep staring." Gwenn's voice brought a wave of heat to my cheeks. "Don't blush, I'm only teasing," she said with a laugh. "I know my brother's pretty hot."

Pretty hot didn't even begin to cover it. Okay, so he was her brother, and she probably didn't see him in that way, but still. Romaric was more than just pretty hot. Any woman would have said he was smoking, and a good number would have given anything to have a shot with him . . .

Including you, a small voice reminded me.

Whoops! In a novel—both the ones I read and the ones I write—the truth always comes from the little voices. Once more, I couldn't disagree with it.

"He looks like you, you know," I told Erwan, trying to change the subject. "He has your eyes. He's the spitting image of your younger self."

Erwan raised an eyebrow, unintentionally making the resemblance even more pronounced. "You think so?"

"You have to show me those articles, Flavie," Gwenn begged. "I want to see the pictures."

"Sure. They're back at the bed-and-breakfast."

I turned to Erwan. "You were very handsome back in the day." He raised an eyebrow again while Gwenn giggled. "I mean—you still are . . . Oh drat, I'll just stop talking!" I burst out laughing too. "For a teacher, I sure am good at putting my foot in my mouth!"

"Don't worry," Erwan assured me, amused. "I understood what you meant. I have to admit I was a looker," he added with a twinkle in his eyes.

"A heartbreaker, you mean!" I told him.

"I doubt it!"

"Maybe you didn't know, but several young girls were madly in love with you. Maybe they never dared to tell you. Maybe . . ."

"Ah, the writer shows her true colors. Wild imagination ruling over fact," Erwan teased.

"I'm sure she's right, Erwan," Gwenn interjected. "You just never realized because only sculpting mattered to you."

Sculpting, and Amélie, I thought.

"Never realized what?" Romaric asked, setting four glasses on our table.

"That he broke many a young lady's vulnerable heart," Gwenn said dramatically.

"I can see you moved on to the heavy stuff while I was gone."

"We had to entertain ourselves somehow. Thanks for the juice. I guess this means there was no alcohol?" Gwenn asked with a sigh.

"Brilliant deduction, Sherlock!" Romaric winked at his sister.

"How much do I owe you?" I asked.

"Not a thing, it's my treat. I don't want to hear any protests," he added as I opened my mouth to do just that, as any good feminist would.

"So what are we drinking to?" Gwenn asked before I could start defending myself.

All gazes turned on me. This family was good at changing subjects.

"All right, and thanks for the drink, Romaric. To life and its surprises."

"To life and its surprises," my three companions repeated.

Romaric's eyes raked across mine as he chimed in.

We drank in silence—or at least the relative silence of the band playing a rock song. My foot started tapping to the beat, and I could feel the urge to dance.

I've always loved to dance. Don't get me wrong, I don't actually know *how* to dance, and I'm pretty sure I don't have a hidden talent for it. Like just about anybody, I can dance to "Macarena" and "Y.M.C.A." and do the Chicken Dance or a conga line. With a decent partner, I can dance to rock'n'roll music or salsa. But dancing opportunities have been pretty scarce these last few years, so that's pretty much the range of my dancing skills.

Romaric must have noticed me moving to the beat because he set his glass down and held a hand out to me. His smile could have melted an iceberg.

"Beautiful lady, may I have this dance?"

The butterflies in my stomach decided to get with the program, jumping straight into their own frenzied dance, but I did my best to ignore them. I made sure my knees weren't going to give if I moved, and I got to my feet, accepting his offer with a teasing reply. "Thank you, sir, that's very kind of you."

Out of the corner of my eye, I saw Erwan hide a smile and share a conspiratorial glance with Gwenn, but Romaric whisked me away before I could think on it any longer. We stepped onto the dance floor and he made me dance like I never had before—he literally made my head spin.

He wasn't an expert dancer—there's no such thing as perfection, though I privately thought that Romaric came pretty close—but he was very good. Better than I was, in any case, and skilled enough that I had no problem following his lead. He moved smoothly, as we spun and twirled until I no longer knew where and who I was. But his gaze never left mine. I could almost believe I was in a *Dirty Dancing* movie scene. The world had ceased to exist beyond our immediate surroundings, and the only real things in it were his hand in mine and our gazes locked together. My heart beat a frantic tattoo, and I was dizzy from the dance and from the closeness of his body when he drew me against his chest with a quick press of his arm and slid his hand into the small of my back.

Song after song flashed by, and still we danced, until I begged for mercy. I was parched and I needed a breather.

We sat down just as the band played the first bars of a slow dance. Part of me wished I could have held on a little longer. I could have been in his arms right now . . . I took a hearty swig of juice to counter my disappointment. Of course, it only made me thirstier.

A pretty young woman—what a surprise!—came up to Romaric and asked him to dance.

"Sorry, I already have a partner," he replied without the slightest hesitation.

I watched as the young woman walked away, disappointed, and I couldn't help rejoicing deep inside. Romaric was here with me! Me! I hid my triumphant smile by taking another gulp of juice and noticed, about a million beats too late, that Gwenn had been invited to dance and that she seemed deep in conversation with her partner. I noticed his hand was rather low on her back, but she didn't seem to mind; on the contrary, I could tell from the way they held themselves that they knew each other. Their movements were cautious, but you could feel the current sparking between them.

Was he the one who had made her smile that night, when she went to *check on the horses*, as she put it?

As always, my natural curiosity almost got the better of me, and I barely stopped myself from asking Romaric, aware that Gwenn's relationship—or lack thereof—with her partner was none of my business. Instead I turned to Erwan, still seated.

"Not dancing, Erwan?"

"The most beautiful lady of the party is already taken, so no."

"Who is it?" I turned back and scanned the dance floor. "Gwenn?"

I heard him laugh and looked back at him. "You, who else?"

"Ooh, what a charmer you are! Romaric, can I have this dance with your uncle?"

He smiled at me and nodded.

"Come on Erwan, let's dance! You promised!"

"Well, your wish is my command." He bowed with a smile.

The band struck up another slow song right as we came up to the dance floor. Out of the corner of my eye, I saw Gwenn stay with her partner. Erwan raised his left hand and slipped the right onto my waist. I put my right hand into his and my left onto his shoulder, and we started to dance.

After a few moments, Erwan spoke. "Can I ask you something, Flavie? Something a bit . . . personal."

"Of course."

"Why did you look for Amélie and me? Why didn't you just throw the letter away? Most people would have. I'm grateful you didn't, don't get me wrong, but I wonder what made you decide to search for us."

"Maybe as a historian, I wanted to know what had become of you and Amélie. Whether life had brought you together in spite of everything . . ."

"Is that all?"

"It was, at least in the beginning."

"What about after?"

"After . . . The further I looked, the more I learned about each of you—well, Amélie, really, because you were harder to track down. Anyway, as I learned more about you, I grew . . . attached. To both of you. Your story . . . called to me. I thought about it all the time. I wanted to know what had happened. I wanted to write about it because I was convinced it had to be a beautiful story. It had to be, even if the ending was a sad one, at least so far. And . . ." I hesitated.

"Yes?"

"Well, I have to admit that I was hoping I'd be the one to reunite you. I know it's kind of forward on my part, but I hoped . . . I don't know. I guess I hoped I could do something good, something that would make people happy for once."

"I'm sure you make people happy every day. Being a teacher requires a lot of dedication."

"Yes, but what I meant is that I wanted to do something real for you. I wanted to be Sam Beckett. You know, the do-gooder doctor of the *Quantum Leap* series," I added when I noticed Erwan's perplexed look. "I wanted to correct the mistakes of the past. Help you find your soul mate again, if you want." I grimaced an apology.

He smiled. "You know, I've thought about what you said. About how it's never too late."

I nodded. "So?"

"I . . . I haven't made a decision yet. I need to think about it some more. I'm . . . I guess I'm a little afraid. Silly, isn't it? I'm almost sixty-three and I'm afraid of a woman I once knew."

"I don't think it's silly at all. I think it means you still love her. If you didn't feel anything for her, you wouldn't be afraid."

"But does she still feel anything for me?"

"I think she does. But that's just my opinion. Listen, I'm not trying to make you do anything. I just want you to know that if you need to talk about it, or anything else, really, I will always be here."

"Thank you, Flavie. Thank you for everything you've done."

"You're welcome, Erwan. I should be the one to thank you—you've welcomed me as if I were a long-lost relative when you had no reason to do so much. I've had a wonderful time, and I'm never going to forget that. I'm never going to forget you."

My eyes found Romaric, watching me dance with his uncle. He smiled at me the way he'd done so often since I'd arrived, and I sighed.

I certainly wasn't going to forget this little trip. I wasn't going to forget Erwan or Gwenn . . . and especially not Romaric. Not a chance!

The last bars of the song faded, and Erwan escorted me back to our table, where he thanked me and delivered me back into the hands of my oh-so-very-handsome partner.

The rest of the evening flew by, and before I knew it, it was almost midnight. My carriage was about to turn back into a pumpkin and this wonderful day was almost at its end. And so was my stay—my heart tightened at the thought.

I had only two days left to enjoy spending time with Romaric, Erwan, and Gwenn. After that, life would call me back to Karouac. I had promised my father I would help him inventory his shop. I knew that if I asked, he would tell me he didn't need my help, but I also knew that I would never ask.

There was a reason my father always did inventory the same week every year. It was his wedding anniversary, and his birthday. Even so many years later, it still was a difficult time for him, and I had promised myself many years ago that I would always be there to help that week. I have never failed to keep that vow, and I wasn't about to start now.

Even if I had to leave the man I had fallen in love with.

I couldn't deny it anymore. I didn't know when or how it had happened, but I had fallen for him headfirst, like a teenager, quickly and irreversibly. It was stupid, given that our lives would soon part, probably forever. We might keep in touch for a few weeks, maybe a couple of months, the way you might with friends you meet on a holiday. And then life would move on, conversations would grow further apart and finally disappear entirely.

My heart tightened at the idea of drifting away from these people I had fallen in love with so fast, too fast perhaps. I didn't want to lose any of them, and especially not Romaric. I really, really didn't want to.

I felt fifteen again, leaving summer camp with a heavy heart.

I couldn't help but sigh, attracting Romaric's attention.

"Are you all right?" he asked, gazing at me.

I felt tears rising and blinked to hold them back. I offered him a guileless smile. "Just fine, thanks."

He opened his mouth to say something, but he was interrupted before he could speak.

"Ladies and gentlemen!" The speaker stood on the music stage. "Fireworks will begin in a few minutes on the beach, and trust me, you don't want to miss that! We'll meet up right after for a big finish with a few last dances!"

As one, the crowd of dancers moved toward the trail leading to the beach, followed by all the people sitting at the tables, as we were. Romaric rose and offered me a hand, and the three of us followed the crowd.

The fireworks were decent enough. Not quite as good as the ones in Karouac, but still very nice. After fifteen minutes of oohing and aahing and an explosive finale, everybody trooped back toward the dance floor.

Luckily, our table had remained empty, but when we reached it, Erwan did not sit down.

"Well, youngsters, my old bones are tired, so I'll head home. Rom, if you see your sister, give her a kiss from me. You two have a good time now. Flavie, will you come over tomorrow?"

"With pleasure!"

"Come around for dinner and bring my nephew and niece along, will you? If you manage to find Gwenn in the meantime."

"Sure!"

He kissed my cheek, then hugged Romaric's shoulders—Rom . . . I loved the nickname!—before he walked back to his car.

The band struck up a slow song, and Romaric—I didn't dare call him Rom without an express invitation to do so—asked for another dance.

I was only too glad to accept.

I had been waiting for this all evening. Heart beating, I slipped into his arms and we started to dance in silence. I loved the feel of his hand, both firm and gentle on my back, the way his cheek hovered just above my hair. I loved the smell of his aftershave—or was it his soap? I wasn't quite sure. I loved the heat rising from his body.

Unconsciously I drew closer until my breasts brushed his chest and I had to resist laying my head on his shoulder. I looked up, met his gaze, and all of a sudden the entire world around us seemed to disappear. I could hear nothing, see nothing but his face bent toward mine and the gentle smile upon his lips. Time had no power over us.

Or so it seemed until the moment the weather decided to get involved. A fat droplet of rain splashed into my right eye, shattering the illusion. I held back a decidedly unfeminine curse and took a step back, rubbing my eye and trying not to smear mascara, which unfortunately was not waterproof. The traitorous raindrop was soon followed by a second, then a third, and before we knew it, the skies opened up, and torrential rain poured over us.

Of course, it was freezing. Where would the fun be otherwise?

"Come on!" Romaric called, trying to make himself heard over the roar of the water. "We have to get out of the rain!"

He pulled me with him, shielding me as best he could from the downpour with his body. Naturally, it wasn't enough and within moments we were drenched and freezing.

We found cover under the porch of a shop, along with several other dancers just as wet as we were. My dress clung to my skin, completely see-through, and nobody could doubt for a second that I was cold. I glued myself to Romaric, hoping he wouldn't notice my raised nipples, and I felt his hand on my back drawing me closer still. There was very little room under the porch, and more and more people were joining us.

Romaric lowered his head and whispered in my ear. "We should run to the car. We'd be drier there!"

"Okay."

There was no way I could get wetter than I already was, and in his car at least we could turn on the heat.

"Let's go!"

We ran to the car. He unlocked it with the fob and we rushed inside, slamming the doors behind us. Romaric immediately started the motor and cranked up the heat.

"What is it they say? It never rains but it pours?" he quipped as he turned to me.

"Yeah, I'm soaked!" I crossed my arms over my chest, hoping he couldn't tell that I might as well have been wearing nothing.

We must have been a fright, our hair plastered to our skulls, clothes clinging to our bodies, absolutely drenched. Unable to resist the humor of our situation, I started giggling, then abandoned all restraint and laughed uncontrollably, soon joined by Romaric. We couldn't stop—every time our gazes crossed we were in stitches again. A long time—or maybe it was only a few minutes, I had lost all track of time—went by before we managed to get our laughter under control, smiling like loons instead.

Then our smiles faded, replaced by something else. A kind of electricity was in the air, something that hadn't been there before, as Romaric kept his gaze on me. Slowly, his hand traveled up my cheek, slid up under my hair. His eyes roamed over my face, from my lips to my eyes and back as he drew almost imperceptibly closer. Our faces were so close together his eyes filled my entire line of sight. I could see only him, smell his scent, hear him breathe. After what seemed like an eternity, his lips met mine, softly at first, a chaste kiss, and I sighed into it. My knees trembled, all of my strength had deserted me, and I could feel shivers up my spine.

And when he laid his other hand on my opposite cheek, opened his mouth and slid his tongue around mine, I lost all sense of reality. His kiss was tender and passionate, gentle and demanding. His tongue stroked mine greedily, slowly, sensually. My hands came up to bury themselves in his hair, and I plunged into the whirlwind of sensations his lips, his hands, and his touch awakened within me.

It was as though a fever had gripped us and set our bodies ablaze, ripping all sense from our minds. Our gentle kiss became more heated. As if in a daze, I could feel his hand exploring my body through my wet dress, stroking my legs, my thighs, my back, my breasts, his mouth peppering thousands of kisses over my skin, our bodies trying to draw closer, to merge together.

As we moved closer together, I found myself straddling his knees, and as I kissed him breathlessly, my hands strayed to the belt of his pants, starting to undo it. It was an awkward position—the steering wheel stopped me from moving the way I wanted—but I didn't care. I wanted Romaric more than anything else in the world, and it was now or never.

I bumped my head on the roof trying to get more comfortable and uttered a low "ouch" of pain.

That stopped Romaric. "Wait! Flavie, wait! Just wait!" His breath was short. He drew back and held me at arm's length, his gaze on mine. "Flavie, wait. We can't do this."

The world seemed to shudder and fall to pieces around me. I should have known. Generally speaking, when it seems too good to be true, it really *is* too good to be true.

"We can't?"

"Not . . . Not here, in the car, like two teenagers. You deserve better than a backseat." He stroked my face, kissed me gently, tenderly. "I have a great bed at home."

"What are we waiting for, then?" My voice was low and throaty. I barely recognized myself.

Romaric kissed me again and helped me into my seat, started up the car, and shifted into drive. He gave me one last kiss, which set my senses on fire—even more than they already were—and drove home far faster than was safe.

We were barely inside the inn before he started kissing me passionately again. I responded eagerly, hardly daring to believe this was happening to me, yet determined to enjoy every minute I spent in his arms. He slid his hands down my back, over my backside and my thighs and lifted me effortlessly. I crossed my legs around his waist and buried my hands in his hair, kissing him all the while. I was vaguely aware of him carrying me into that part of the house I had not visited previously, but I didn't pay much attention to my surroundings. I was focused on Romaric, his hands on my skin, his tongue inside my mouth.

At first, our lovemaking was fast and hard, intense and passionate, fulfilling an imperious need, the insatiable hunger of each other's bodies. The same fire, the same ardor filled us, clamoring to be sated immediately. His hands and his lips were all over my body, tasting every inch, exploring every curve, setting me ablaze, playing with my every nerve until I could only feel my burning desire for Romaric.

Impatient, I slipped the condom on him myself, dragging my hands just a tiny bit longer than strictly necessary in order to drive him crazy—and me along him. His eyelashes fluttered and his breathing shortened as he drew me into his arms. I burrowed closer, ever closer, eager for the soft friction of his body against mine, inside, around, and over me. Body against body, skin against skin, I could feel his heart beat against my ribs, or maybe it was mine beating against his, I couldn't tell. We were as one, and I would have been at pains to say where I stopped and where he began. Slowly, our movements became more urgent, our kisses more passionate, until everything exploded around me and inside me. And from the fog of pleasure, I could feel Romaric following suit.

Later, once we had satisfied our hunger, abated the first frenzied rush, we took the time to explore each other, taste each other, love each other slowly, so slowly, softly and tenderly, by the light of the candles we'd lit. Our gestures were gentler, yet more daring. My hands traveled over the length of Romaric's body, lingering over the muscles in his arms and his stomach, and I delighted in the shivers my touch caused as they trailed over his skin. I slowly awakened his desire and mine again, one kiss at a time, searching for the most sensitive, most erogenous places, testing his resistance and mine until my blood was on fire again and my body craved only one thing: him.

The second time, we made love as though the world outside the walls of his room had disappeared. As though nothing mattered except for our breath mingling, our bodies loving each other, our hearts beating as one.

As though time, which I was running out of, no longer existed.

Chapter 15

The rain had stopped and sunlight tickled my eyelids when I woke up the next morning. I blinked, not quite sure where I was. I certainly hadn't fallen asleep in my usual bed, and neither the arm thrown over me or the hand resting on my left breast were mine. I came awake suddenly as I remembered the previous night.

The party. The rain. The kiss.

And the most heated night of my life.

Now, I'm no blushing virgin. I've had several relationships over the years, some more serious than others, some shorter, some more satisfying. But never anything quite as shattering as last night.

God, how the ground had given way beneath my feet!

Happiness bubbled inside me. I felt very much in love. Any lingering doubts had been thoroughly erased.

I loved him. And yes, I realized it was stupid of me to fall in love under these circumstances. I knew I had to leave in two days and that this wasn't going to be easy. But I hadn't been able to help myself. I couldn't, wouldn't resist. To hell with the consequences, I'd rather live through the experience, follow this story to the end, even if it meant I returned home with a broken heart and buckets of tears. I would not hold back and miss out on such blissful happiness. I had followed Erwan's example. I'd rather love and suffer for it, even for a short time, than protect myself and mourn the opportunity later on. This was worth it. Romaric was worth it.

He was amazing, considerate, thoughtful, passionate, funny, and attractive. So very, very attractive. A woman would have to be either ice-cold or plain crazy to be able to resist him.

And I was neither.

I let out a deep sigh, and slowly turned around to gaze appreciatively at Romaric's naked body. He was still fast asleep, and the sheet had slipped down to sit low on his waist, exposing his perfect body—and mine, which I hastily covered up, blushing like a newly-wed. For a few moments, I admired the gentle curve of his back, the two dimples below his waist. Unable to resist, I brushed the tip of a finger down his arm, still thrown possessively over me, and followed the shape of his spine, hesitating as I reached the barrier of the sheet.

"Don't stop," he breathed.

Blushing, I removed my hand and redirected my gaze toward Romaric's face. He was watching me, amused, the hint of a smile on his lips.

His right hand still lay on my breast.

"Sorry, I didn't want to wake you—" I stopped, unsure what to say to him. What could you say to the man you've fallen madly in love with, the man who just gave you a night the kind you only find in a romance novel? *Hi, how're you doing? Sleep well? Look, I hope you have no regrets because this was the best night of my life and I really, really hope it won't be the only one?* No way.

Apparently, Romaric had no such qualms.

Still smiling, he leaned onto an elbow, and reached out to gently cradle my face with one hand.

"How can I complain when I wake up next to such a beautiful woman?" he murmured as he kissed me languidly.

I felt myself blush with pleasure and sigh in relief. At least he didn't seem to regret anything. One worry out of the way . . .

"Hey, you," he quipped, his mouth barely an inch from my lips.

"Hey, yourself," I answered without moving.

"Sleep well?"

"Mm. Great, thanks."

He smiled and pressed another, deeper kiss to my mouth.

I shifted closer to him, melting into his arms. It was the best place in the entire bed. Interpreting—quite accurately—my gesture as an invitation, he started trailing light kisses up my cheek until he reached that sensitive spot just behind my ear. A shiver ran all over me as a gentle heat started to swell inside me, pooling in my lower belly.

"Flavie?" he whispered into my ear.

"Mm?" I murmured, distracted by the feel of his lips on my skin.

"I spent a wonderful night," he confided, and as though to emphasize this statement, he nibbled at my ear, eliciting a low moan from my throat.

"Me too," I managed to gasp in spite of my brain experiencing major system failure.

He went on for a few more seconds, and just as I was starting to lose all touch with reality, he spoke up.

"Flavie?"

"Mm?" I moaned once again, unable to manage anything better.

How on earth did he expect me to maintain speech functions while his hand stroked my breast, my belly—and occasionally ventured lower—and his mouth tortured my earlobe in such an exquisite fashion?

"Any plans for the next two hours?" he asked, never ceasing his ministrations.

"Not...as far...as I know..."

"Perfect."

He set about outlining his own plans in *very* explicit detail...

It was two hours later by the time hunger drew us out of his room. I went back to my room and showered and threw on some fresh clothes while he cooked us breakfast. When I joined him downstairs, the kitchen smelled like freshly made waffles and my stomach made its presence known rather loudly.

"Sorry about that." I grimaced, patting my stomach. "I think I'm hungry."

"Sit down, I'm almost done."

I sat at the table and he started setting out enough to feed an army. Bread, butter, jam, waffles, tea, and coffee. A rose from the garden in a vase. And on the plate in front of me, he had deposited the adorable bear cub he had been carving the day before while I napped.

"Oh! You finished it!"

"Yes, after we got home yesterday and before we left for the party. It's for you."

"For me? Oh, thank you, I love it! But why?"

"Why not? It's my pleasure."

I cradled the wooden bear in my hands, unable to hold back the smile creeping across my face. "Thank you! It's adorable."

He leaned down and kissed me gently, whispering, "Just like you."

My heart swelled in my chest and, just like that, I fell even more in love with him—if that was possible.

He poured hot water into my cup of tea, coffee into his, and sat next to me.

"Is Gwenn home?" I asked, reaching out to grab a slice of bread and spread jam over it.

"I don't think so. I didn't see her shoes or her car. Good thing nobody was at the bed-and-breakfast last night!"

Just then, the door opened.

"Speak of the devil," Romaric commented. "Is this the time you get home?" he teased her.

"Hello to you too," Gwenn exclaimed as she sat opposite her brother. "And hi, Flavie."

She was still wearing yesterday's clothes and she positively beamed. Apparently her night had been interesting too.

"How're things? Had a good night? I'm starving. Is there enough for me?"

"Sure," I said. "There's more than enough for three. Help yourself!"

She got up to grab a mug from the cupboard and Romaric poured her some coffee, which she downed at once.

She sighed. "God, that tastes good!"

"So." Romaric had donned the protective-big-brother look I had seen on his face once or twice before. "Where were you, anyway?"

I really liked that part of him. How protective he was toward the people he loved. I found it heartwarming.

Yes, I had it bad, and I didn't even care anymore.

"None of your business," Gwenn retorted. "Do I ever ask you who you spend *your* nights with?"

I could feel myself blush, and tried to hide by burying my nose into my cup of tea. It probably was better if she didn't ask who Romaric had spent the night with. I would die of embarrassment.

I think that was the exact moment Gwenn understood something had happened between her brother and me. She looked at my blushing face, then at her brother, back at me, and finally at her brother again, before a knowing smile stretched across her lips.

"Well, I'll change, then go take care of the stables," she said, pouring herself some more coffee and stealing a waffle as she stood up and headed out of the kitchen.

"By the way, Flavie . . ." She turned around just as she was about to exit the room.

"Yeah?"

"Remember how you were supposed to show me how to bind off stitches?"

"Whenever you want," I told her.

The knowing grin was back. "Forget about it. I think you will have better things to do over the next two days . . ."

"Oh, er . . . You sure?"

"Absolutely. We'll see about that some other time."

"Okay, then."

"And anyway, I have my own plans . . ." Her smile was conniving.

Romaric called her back just as she left. "Erwan's invited all of us for dinner tonight!"

"I'll be there!" she hollered in return. "As soon as I've greeted our guests and helped them settle their horses."

She poked her head back into the room. "Have a nice day. And have fun!" Her grin was positively filthy.

"Thanks!"

"See you this evening." And she clicked away on her high heels.

Romaric looked from the door to me and back for a few seconds, then he jumped up and ran after his sister, calling over his shoulder, "Stay there. I'll just be a moment!"

"Er . . . Okay then."

Two minutes later, I had barely finished my toast when he reentered the room, smiling like the cat that got the cream.

"Gwenn's going to run the bed-and-breakfast today. I am free and ready to spend the next two days with you. What do you want to do? Your choice!"

I knew exactly what I wanted. "Take me anywhere you want to, as long as you can tell me a story about it."

"I know just the place."

Chapter 16

As it happened, Romaric really did have the perfect place. The empty ruins of a medieval castle—he was starting to know me quite well!—nestled high on a rocky overhang in the midst of a tree-filled valley, accessible by a long and winding road. It was one of those deserted castles, dating back a long, long time that one can find in countries like France, Italy, and Scotland, just standing there, abandoned and in ruins, full of history and legends and tragedies and love stories. I've always been fascinated by those places, regretting that nobody seemed interested enough to restore them—or rich enough to save them from their inevitable destruction. And this one was no exception. It was beautiful, and its mysterious atmosphere intrigued me as soon as I stepped out of the car.

"Wow," I whispered.

"Flavie, may I present to you Le Château du Val d'Amour?"

The Castle of the Valley of Love. Even the very name of the castle was romantic. How could I resist? "It's breathtaking. I love it."

Romaric laughed softly and threaded his fingers through mine, pulling me behind him.

"Trust me, you haven't seen anything yet. Come on, follow me."

We passed the fortifications and entered the courtyard. I stopped and spun on the spot, feasting my eyes on my surroundings. I couldn't get enough. "This is incredible! I never expected there could be such a place in the middle of the forest!"

"Come on," Romaric insisted. "Have a look inside. There's something I want to show you."

I trailed after him, craning my head this way and that, eager to see everything. He led me down the main hall, up a winding staircase to the next floor, where we moved down a corridor and through another room before he stopped in front of a hole in the wall.

"What's this?" I asked. "A secret passage?"

"Exactly!"

"You're joking." My eyes opened wide. "For real?"

"Absolutely. It leads down the hill, to a cave next to a stream. It's not an easy stroll, but it's perfectly doable and safe."

"You've been there?"

He nodded, laughing at my excitement.

"Wow! A real secret passage! That's amazing!" I paused, watching the dark passage, itching to go and see, although not daring to ask. "How did you ever find this place?" I said instead, out of curiosity. "The castle, I mean. It's so secluded!"

"Erwan worked here one summer, when I was a teenager. To keep me occupied, he took me with him, to help."

"Erwan worked here? What was he doing?"

"He was carving stone blocks to restore the fortifications of the castle."

"Why did he stop?" I asked, frowning.

The castle had obviously not been totally restored.

"They cut the budget, and they had to drop the project."

"That's sad."

"Yeah." Then his eyes seemed to gleam with mischief, and a smile appeared on his lips as he took a flashlight from the inside pocket of his jacket, and waved it at me. "Want to go down?"

"I thought you would never ask!!"

The secret passage—which really wasn't much of a secret, since the hole in the wall was open for all to see—was damp, cold, and narrow, and would have been very, very dark, had Romaric not brought a flashlight. But for all that, I enjoyed every second of the way, picturing the inhabitants of the castle creeping down the passageway to escape a siege or to have a secret meeting with a friend, a lover, a spy. In my mind's eye, I spun romantic and dramatic stories, love stories featuring knights, battles, and treason, filling in what I knew with what I could see around me. At last, after some fifteen minutes' descent, the passageway came to an end, opening into a cave by a riverbed, just as Rom had said.

I just stood there, a silly smile on my face.

It felt as though I was in a Nancy Drew detective novel, and I loved it. "Have you been down here often?" My voice echoed in the cave, multiplying my words by ten.

"Here, as in the cave or the castle?"

"Both," I replied.

"I've been to the castle maybe a dozen times, with Erwan. As to the cave . . ." He smiled softly, a nostalgic smile, as if being there brought back long forgotten memories. "I did wind up here a few times. I discovered the passage on my second trip to the castle." He grimaced. "You should have seen Erwan when I came back up the first time. He'd been looking for me and he was getting seriously worried. I was in for it that day!"

"But he didn't forbid you from going back?" I asked.

"He came down with me."

"I should have guessed as much."

"And when he realized the whole place wasn't about to fall on my head, he let me go back as long as I told him where I was going and I didn't make him late."

"That was pretty lenient of him. I would have grounded you for life if I were him. I'd have been too afraid of something happening to you."

"There's nothing to be afraid of," he said, closing his arms around me. "See?"

"Yeah, okay. Have you come back since?"

"Since the project was canceled, you mean?"

I nodded.

"Never," he said.

"Why not?"

"Never had the chance. Erwan had stopped working there when the next holidays came, so I had no transportation. And after that, I was busy with school, then university, the bed-and-breakfast and all that jazz, so I kind of forgot about it. I remembered it this morning."

"Well, thanks for bringing me here. I love it."

"I knew you would. Can you imagine the things that must have happened here?"

"Perfectly well. People fleeing the castle . . ."

"Secret trysts . . ."

"Clandestine food supplying . . ."

"A lover spirited away . . ."

"Espionage, treason . . ."

Our gazes met and we burst out laughing. We were hopeless. Give us two minutes and we'd rewrite the castle's entire history!

Rom dropped a kiss on my lips. "Want to stay a while longer or go back up?"

"Can we visit the rest of the castle?"

"Your wish is my command, m'lady."

Once we were back in the castle, Romaric took me through each room. It didn't take very long, since the castle was completely empty and, all things considered, rather small.

I sat on the bottom step of the stone stairs leading up to the second floor when we were done, unwilling to leave so soon. Gazing up at the ceiling of what must have been the castle's great hall, I turned to Romaric.

"Tell me the story of this place."

He smiled. "You're going to love it. Very little is known about this castle. Nobody knows when it was built or who exactly lived in it. Historians haven't found a lot of documents mentioning it, even in what remains of the archives of the time, maps or literature. It's a true mystery castle. You're free to imagine whatever happened here."

He fell silent and I waited, certain there had to be something else.

"Of course," he continued, "there are dozens of legends about the castle, its origins and its inhabitants, and everyone has their favorite. But they're just legends, nothing more."

"What kind of legends?"

"Some say that the castle was built by a battle-weary knight back from the Crusades. He never wanted to hear of war again, so he decided to live away from the rest of the world. Other stories have it that this was where great lords of Brittany kept their mistresses."

"But you don't believe that."

He shook his head. "There's something about the atmosphere here that makes me want to believe in another legend."

"What's your favorite?"

He sat next to me, leaning against the wall, and pulled me toward him. I went willingly, laying my head on his shoulder and preparing to be lulled by his voice.

"Once upon a time," he began, lazily running a finger down my arm, "there was a young stable boy named Youenn. He was a simple person, kind and caring. He was devoted to the lord he served and would have gladly laid down his life for him. This lord had a daughter, Alwenn, of unsurpassed beauty. One day, she was abducted by a rival lord and locked away for weeks. Her father was beside himself with worry. Ever since his wife had died, his daughter was all that he had left in this world, and he spared no expense to rip her from his enemy's claws. He sent entire armies of knights, but they all trudged back empty-handed.

"But Youenn had an idea. He had loved Alwenn long and true, and one night, he crept out of the castle, disguised as one of the enemy's servants. After a few weeks of dedicated effort, he was assigned the honor of bringing Alwenn her meals. She recognized him instantly despite the disguise, and understood that he was there to save her. Her courage revived, she prepared for her rescue. It was difficult for Youenn to find the right moment, but at last, several nights later, he found a way to get her out and brought her back to the castle as fast as his stolen horse could get them, and very humbly returned her to her father's arms.

"The lord saw how Youenn looked at her, and knew his love to be true. He raised him to a knight, telling the king that Youenn had shown more wit and courage than many a knight he knew. Secretly, with the help of the fairies and their magic, he had this castle built. When it was finished, he asked his daughter whether she loved Youenn. Alwenn blushed and admitted that she dearly loved Youenn and wished nothing more than to marry him. Now certain of his daughter's feelings, the lord told Alwenn that he would be happy to welcome Youenn into his family. On their wedding day, he gave them this castle so they might live in safety to the end of their days . . ."

I sighed deeply. "What a beautiful story . . . It's my favorite too."

"You haven't heard the others yet."

"It doesn't matter. You've told it so well no other can compare."

Rom dropped a kiss on my hair and tightened his grip on me.

I turned toward him. "How do you know all this? All these legends, all these stories . . . you know more than I do, yet I was the one studying history."

"That's not quite true. I took some cultural inheritance classes at the same time as my econ ones. I wanted to be able to tell my customers about the places to see around here, and for that, I needed to know everything about the region. I read all I could find about local curiosities, folktales, and places of interest in the history books and the tourist guides. Anything within fifty kilometers of our place."

He would never cease to surprise me. "Wow."

"Are you impressed?"

He said it teasingly, mock-proud, but I was honestly impressed. I told him so, and his face lit up.

"Do I get brownie points?"

"A few. Maybe even a lot."

"I see." He thought about it for a few seconds. "If I told you the tragic and fascinating story of the woman who lived in the bed-and-breakfast during World War One, do you think I could convince you to—"

He cut himself off.

"To?" I insisted.

He whispered into my ear.

"Really." I arched a teasing eyebrow. "That's a tall order, Mr. Kermarrec. Do you really think I would go along with such a thing?"

"There's only one way to find out, Miss Richalet. So," he asked, gently rubbing his nose against mine and dropping one kiss, then a second and a third on my lips, "how about it, Professor? Will you accept my request?"

"Your story had better be a good one if you want me to consider the challenge met and your request granted," I whispered as I kissed him back. "You're going to have to impress me even more. I'm grading on a steep curve."

"Believe me, Miss Richalet, I'll impress you . . . Really impress you . . ."

"Show-off."

Chapter 17

"All right, dear family." Gwenn was out of her chair almost before she'd swallowed her last mouthful. "Sorry for the dine-and-dash routine, but I have plans for tonight."

Rom's face immediately assumed is protective-big-brother expression. "Where are you going?"

"Not that it's any of your business, but I'm off to see Dan. We're going to the fair."

"His name is Dan?"

Gwenn arched an eyebrow. Her resemblance to Romaric had never been as pronounced as it was in that instant.

"Yes, his name is Dan." She sighed, exasperated. "He's my age, he does karate, so I should be perfectly safe with him. Any other questions?"

"Um . . . No. Just be careful, all right?"

"Don't worry, brother mine." Gwenn softened and kissed her brother's cheek. "I'll be careful. No need to fret."

"I know, but . . . Yeah. Have fun."

"You too!"

Gwenn kissed Erwan, then me, before she left the house.

Erwan considered his nephew for a few moments. "One day you'll have to accept that she's a big girl and she doesn't need you to look after her."

Rom sighed. "I know. I just can't help worrying."

"Leave her alone. She's big enough to know what she's doing. And she deserves to meet someone nice who'll take care of her."

"How do you know he's nice and will take care of her?"

"I have my sources."

"See? You talk about how overprotective I am, but you're really no better!"

"Except I'm more discreet."

I held back a smile. The apple never fell far from the tree, and Erwan and Romaric were even more similar than I had thought at first. Both were considerate and thoughtful, kind and loving, and very protective. They both watched very closely over the ones they loved. And just like Amélie back in the day, I was unable to resist such a nearly perfect man.

"We'll be taking our leave too, Erwan. Flavie owes me a walk on the beach."

That wasn't quite what I owed him, but obviously, Rom couldn't tell his uncle the exact nature of what I had promised to do if his story was as good as he'd sworn it was.

And believe me, it had been—better, in fact. It had been so beautiful, so touching and tender, so dramatic and filled with passion, so heartbreaking that one day I would probably write that woman's story.

But in the meantime, I had a deal to make good on. A promise made is a promise owed.

"Go ahead. Have fun!"

"Good night, Erwan. See you tomorrow," I said as I kissed his cheek. I had almost come to think of him as my own uncle.

Then I followed Romaric.

Smiling softly, Erwan brewed himself a pot of coffee and after pouring some into a mug, he sipped it, sitting on the terrace.

This evening was a happy one. Both his nephew and niece, the people he loved most in the world, had met their special someone. It might be a little early to tell if Gwenn's boyfriend was the one, but he hadn't seen her so happy in a long time.

Romaric was another story.

He was falling fast and hard for Flavie, Erwan could tell. He had never seen his nephew as happy as he was since Flavie had come into their lives.

She was perfect for him. She was kind and gentle and obviously head over heels for him too, which was a serious point in her favor.

You'd have to be blind to miss it—every time she looked at Romaric, her eyes lit up with a very specific flame.

The very same he saw in his nephew's eyes.

They hadn't spoken about it, but Erwan knew his nephew well and it was impossible to misunderstand the subtle signals Romaric was giving off. He was falling in love with the woman who had changed his uncle's life.

Erwan set his mug down and reached for the letter he had been carrying in his pocket ever since he'd gotten it back. He gazed at it for a long while, making no move to unfold it.

Flavie had changed his life when she'd returned this letter. She had given him new purpose, and she had given him hope. Hope that there still might be a chance for Amélie and him.

Her words rang out in his mind. *Everything can be changed. Only death is forever. And even that is negotiable. Just look at Orpheus.*

It had made him think, and he was considering more and more seriously the idea of finding Amélie again, if only to talk to her, so they could explain to each other what had happened back then. To find out whether all hope was lost or if she might one day forgive him for not doing enough to find her.

Yes. With each passing day, his way seemed clearer and clearer.

He had to know, to decide.

Was this worth risking all hope?

"Well, Miss Richalet, I think it's time for you to fulfill your end of the deal."

"Here?" I asked, casting an eye around.

We had entered a lovely little cove, calm and peaceful, bathed in soft moonlight. The only drawback—which was also its main asset that evening—was that it was difficult to reach. We'd had to climb a long stretch of rock that circled around the beach and hid the cove from passersby, creating a small private space for anyone who knew it was there. It was almost midnight, and we were alone, the silence around us broken only by the slow rush of the waves and the ocean breeze, the only light coming from the moon and the flashlight we had used to climb the rocks. I could almost believe we were the only people in the world.

"This is the perfect place!" Romaric declared as he dug a large blanket out of his rucksack and spread it over the ground. "Nobody is going to walk in on us here!"

I hesitated.

"Having second thoughts, Professor?" He raised a provoking eyebrow.

"Absolutely not," I retorted. "I'm ... I'm thinking."

"About what?"

"What I'm going to take off first."

"Mmm, this is getting interesting ..."

I took a deep breath and started taking my clothes off. Shawl, right sandal, left sandal, watch, earrings, T-shirt, skirt, they all came off slowly, as sensually as I could manage. I saw his gaze heat up, and when I stepped out of my skirt, I could have sworn he was about to pull me into his arms.

But the challenge wasn't over yet. I slowly backed away until the waves lapped at my heels, never breaking eye contact. The cold made me shiver, but I kept moving until the water was waist-deep. I dove below the surface and took off my underwear and bra. Shaking the water out of my eyes, I threw them onto the beach.

They fell at Romaric's feet, which had not been my intention—I had been aiming for the blanket, but my throwing arm had never been that great. Romaric looked down upon them wordlessly for a few moments.

"Who's having second thoughts now?"

"Certainly not me!" he hastened to reply as he took off his own clothes.

Including his underwear.

Gulp.

It was the first time I'd seen him in all his naked glory from afar. Of course, I knew his body. I'd explored every centimeter avidly last night, but he was so beautiful, so handsome, that watching him was like looking at a painting from some great artist, a never-ending joy, an addictive performance you simply could not get enough of. As he walked toward me, I took pleasure in admiring every muscle, every curve, every line of his body. Despite the darkness, he must have noticed my lustful gaze, because a naughty smile appeared on his lips and he slowed his pace markedly, letting me feast my eyes on him.

When he did reach me, I immediately went to him and curled up in his arms. Partly because I hoped it would hide the fact that I wasn't completely at ease being stark naked in the open—even if nobody was there—but mostly because right then, I wanted, no, needed, to feel him against me. I had just spent the entire day with him, a day which would stay with me forever: wonderful, extraordinary, unforgettable . . . but the fateful moment when I'd have to say goodbye had also drawn one day closer. And God knows I wasn't ready for that.

Instinctively, I closed my arms around him, holding him tight as though to mark my skin with his forever.

"Hey," he said, looking worried, cradling my face in his hands. "Are you okay?"

"Yeah, I'm okay. Fine." I tried to muster a convincing smile. "Not completely at ease, that's all."

Smiling, he tugged me farther in, until the water reached my shoulders.

"Better?"

"A little, yes."

He lifted me up and guided my legs around his waist, holding me close. I could feel his fever-hot skin against mine, my breasts against his chest, his lower belly pressing against mine.

"How about now?" he asked, his face an inch from mine, our noses bumping. "Feel better?"

My blood began to pump faster as I started to forget where I was. "A little."

"Just a little?" he insisted, dropping a kiss onto my lips and rolling his hips ever so slightly.

Just enough for me to feel it, and for heat to start rising up inside me. "Mmm . . ."

"Is there anything I can do to put you more at ease?"

His lips had found my ear, my neck, my shoulder, and his hips kept rolling slowly, a barely perceptible rocking, just enough to drive me crazy. Instinctively, my back arched.

"Maybe," I breathed.

"Tell me."

My lips brushed against his ear. "Love me," I whispered.

And he did.

His eyes on mine, shining with an intense fire that never failed to set me ablaze, he pulled me back to the beach and, kissing me all the while, he laid me down on the blanket and reached for a condom.

Then he loved me. Tenderly and reverently, gently and passionately, whispering sweet words into my ear, repeating my name against my lips, stifling my cries with his kisses, giving me exactly what I had asked for—the feeling that, just for a few moments, tomorrow no longer existed.

Later, when our bodies had been sated, when our heartbeats had started winding back to normal and our breath had slowed, Romaric's gaze met mine. He kissed me slowly and sweetly and, laying his forehead against mine, spoke the words I had both hoped for and feared.

"Stay. Don't leave yet."

I closed my eyes and sighed. "I can't," I whispered.

"Oh," he said, drawing away slightly.

I couldn't stand the disappointment in his voice, echoing what I felt inside. I took his face in my hands, forcing him to meet my eyes. I wanted to explain. I wanted him to understand.

"I want to stay, Rom. That's not the problem. But my father's wedding anniversary is coming up as well as his birthday and... ever since my mother left, it's always been a difficult time of the year for him." I paused. "It's important that I be there for him that day, see? I can't not be. Leaving you is the last thing I want to do, and it gets more difficult by the minute, but . . . ."

"Don't worry," he replied. "I understand. I understand," he repeated more softly.

His arms grew tighter around me.

"We'll figure something out," he whispered, kissing me softly and sweetly, in that special way of his that always made me shiver. "I promise we'll figure something out."

Chapter 18

Two days later

"Knock knock."

I looked up from my packing to see Romaric leaning against the open door to my room.

"Hey," I said with a sad little smile.

"Hey, yourself."

We stared at each other in silence for a few moments, then Romaric spoke up.

"Flavie..." He stopped and suddenly strode across the room, reaching out to cradle my face between his hands and kiss me. I closed my eyes, as much to savor the feeling of his lips on mine as to hold back my tears.

The kiss was both gentle and desperate, and it spoke volumes about how much he was going to miss me.

Me too, Rom. I'm going to miss you. So, so much.

Too soon, he drew away from me and gently laid his forehead against mine. "Drive safe, okay?"

"Promise," I whispered, my voice hoarse with unshed tears.

"Call me when you get home?"

"I will. As soon as I arrive."

It was the best compromise we'd been able to work out. Phone calls. Skype. Any kind of long-distance communication.

We'd talked about it at length the day before. Romaric had even suggested inviting my father to come and spend some time up here. It was an enticing idea, as it would have postponed the moment we'd have to part, and so I was grateful to Romaric for being willing to welcome my father into his home. But I also knew Papa better than anyone else, and I knew he would refuse, arguing that he couldn't close shop in the middle of the summer, even for just a few days. It was the best time of the year for his business, and though a few days away wouldn't bankrupt him, it was true that it would make a difference. Then he'd probably insist I stay and enjoy myself rather than bother with the shop or his birthday, let alone his wedding anniversary. No doubt he would add that it was high time I started living my own life without worrying about my old father, and that he got along just fine, thank you.

But although it was true, I didn't want him to have to. For years it had been just the two of us. He'd leaned on me as I had on him. How could I leave him alone when I knew my mother's desertion still hurt, even after all these years, and that my presence by his side was one of the only things that would stop him from dwelling on painful memories all week? I couldn't, and that was that. Romaric hadn't insisted, knowing that he would do the same for Erwan if the situation called for it.

We'd been through every possible scenario and in the end, we'd had to decide that for now, phone calls would have to be enough.

I closed my eyes, barely clamping down on a sigh of despair.

Despite coming to an agreement, my heart had been filled with anxiety for the last day or so. I'd made every effort to be as rational as I could and keep my cool, but I still couldn't get rid of the niggling sensation that today was the last I'd see of him, the last time I'd feel his heart beat against mine. The last time I'd touch him, the last time we'd kiss.

The mere idea was enough to send me spiraling into a pit of despair. My heart felt as though it was slowly turning to ash, crumbling under the weight of my fears.

What if our story turned out to be just a summer fling, intense but short-lived? What if, in spite of all our promises, we never met again? What if life, prior commitments, routine, finally doused the flames?

What if... what if his feelings for me weren't quite as strong as mine were?

Would I survive?

I plunged my gaze deep into his, searching and hoping against hope to find the certainty that my fears, and the bitter taste in my mouth, were unfounded.

That our story would endure and go on.

But deep down, I knew that he could make me no such promise. Even the most earnest of good intentions could only carry you so far. I was painfully aware that we had each built a life that we loved and would have difficulty leaving behind. Romaric had his bed-and-breakfast, his horses, his sister, and his uncle; I had my house, my students, my father, and my friends. Two lives, two jobs, two different realities that kept us apart just as much as they had brought us together.

I didn't know whether our strength of will would be enough to overcome these obstacles, whether we'd be strong enough to compromise as needed, whether the situation would slowly become unbearable until it heralded the end of the *us* I so desperately craved and I could already feel slipping away . . .

I drew back before I could burst into tears—or do something truly stupid such as telling him that I loved him, that over the last few days I had fallen head over heels for him, which I refused to do because our situation was complicated enough, and I didn't want him to feel pressured.

With all the depressing thoughts circling in my mind, chasing away all other considerations, it was utter heartbreak. It must have been the hardest thing I had done in a long time, or maybe ever.

Immediately I felt empty.

Get used to it, honey, you're in it for the long haul!

I gave Romaric my best quivering smile, trying to tamp down the myriad emotions inside of me, and discreetly wiped away the tear I hadn't been able to hold back.

"I hate goodbyes," I griped. "Really. Whoever invented those, worst idea ever!"

I knew the joke wouldn't quite be enough to ease the tension, but I needed some humor so I wouldn't start sobbing out loud then and there.

"Me too," Romaric said, a humorless smile on his lips. "And today more than ever."

I turned my back to him, as much to finish packing as to conceal my trembling hands and lips. I took my time to put away my computer, shifting it this way and that, checking and double-checking it wouldn't slip, closing the zipper at a snail's pace. At last, there was nothing left to do to delay the inevitable, and I took a deep breath before turning toward him.

"I'm ready," I claimed with as much conviction as I could.

"I'll carry your suitcase down."

"Thanks."

Outside, Gwenn and Erwan were waiting for me. I let Romaric put my suitcase and backpack into the car, and deposited my handbag on the passenger seat. I turned to Gwenn first and hugged her tight.

"Thanks for everything, Gwenn. For being so kind, so welcoming, for lending me your riding outfit. It really was great meeting you."

"Same here." She hugged me back. "Be careful on the road, okay? Call us when you get home."

"Promise."

"And Skype us when you have a minute."

"I will. Gladly. And I know I've already said this, but if you ever want to come to the northern coast, I have a guest bedroom . . . with a double bed." I winked. "In case you want to bring company."

"That's so sweet of you! Careful, I might take you up on that offer."

"Please. I'd love to take you to my knitting circle and introduce you to the girls. I know you'd get along very well."

"Okay, now I just have to visit. Don't know when, but you can definitely expect me!"

She tightened her embrace, then released me and stepped back so I could face Erwan.

"Erwan." I put my arms around him. "Thank you for everything. For telling me your story. I'll be forever grateful that you let a perfect stranger into your home and your heart."

"You're welcome." He hugged me back. "But you're not a stranger anymore. You haven't been for quite some time."

"Thanks, Erwan. Rom and Gwenn are really lucky to have an uncle like you. You're welcome at my place too, anytime. And in any case, you're not getting rid of me that easily. I still have a story to write."

"I certainly hope so." He smiled and lowered his voice. "Speaking of which . . . If, say, I decided to heed your advice and go south . . . Would you . . . Would you come with me?"

Astounded, I stepped back, eyes wide.

"Don't get your hopes up, I haven't reached a decision yet. I'm just asking."

A wide smile split my face in two. *Yes!* "Nothing would give me greater pleasure, Erwan."

"Because really, if you're going to write this story . . . Well, it needs an ending, doesn't it?"

My heart swelled with happiness. If Erwan found Amélie again . . . If they got to talk to each other and explain . . . If their story managed to pick up where it left off . . . I would be so happy for him! It would almost make up for the heartbreak I was currently feeling.

Almost.

"Of course!" I said enthusiastically. "A story with no ending makes no sense. You need an ending."

"Yes, well. As I said, I haven't decided yet."

"Yes, yes, of course. But . . . you know where to find me when you've made up your mind."

"I do."

I hugged him one last time before I stepped back, and he smiled down on me.

"You be careful now, Flavie."

"Thank you, Erwan."

I could feel myself tearing up again and I blinked hard.

"Gwenn, didn't you want to show me something in the stables?" Erwan asked, his gaze heavy with meaning.

She frowned, but quickly caught on. "Oh yeah, sure. Come along!"

I smiled, not fooled in the slightest. They were giving Romaric and me privacy to say our goodbyes. I was starting to hate that word.

We watched them walk away arm in arm before we turned back to face each other.

"Okay. This is it. I . . ."

I couldn't finish. Romaric had thrown his arms around me and kissed me with raw and desperate hunger. I kissed him back just as desperately, with the same regret.

"Flavie," he muttered.

"Don't . . . don't say anything, all right? Tell me later. When I call you. Okay? Let me believe this isn't forever."

"It—"

I laid a finger across his lips. I didn't want to hear what he had to say. Like Amélie before me, I refused to chain the man I loved with promises he might not be able to keep. I'd rather he stayed silent than swore the impossible.

Even if my heart raged at the thought.

"Shhh." I dropped one last kiss on his lips, trying to express all my pain, my frustration, my fear. Then I tore away from him, climbed into the car, and sped out of the courtyard as though the hounds of hell were chasing me, unmindful of the silent tears running down my face.

I never looked back. My heart had shattered already.

A few meters away, Erwan turned back and watched Flavie streak away, his heart aching on his nephew's behalf; he knew what it felt like to part with someone you loved. It hurt. A lot.

He looked at Romaric, who seemed lost, uncertain, as though the entire world had stopped.

"He's going to miss her," Gwenn said softly beside him.

"I know."

"And so will I. I really like her."

"Me too. But it's only goodbye for now, not forever," Erwan murmured.

"I hope so." Gwenn looked speculatively at her uncle.

"You can certainly do better than just hope. We'll be seeing her in a few weeks. I have a plan," Erwan said.

"A plan? I'm all ears."

"I'm going to find Amélie. With you and Rom—and Flavie will be coming with us."

Chapter 19

I couldn't stay still.

I was unable to sit or read. I couldn't knit more than a couple of stitches before I had to get up and peer through the window to see whether he was here yet.

I was like a little kid waiting for Santa Claus. Except I wasn't waiting for the jolly fat guy.

I was waiting for *him*.

I left my post to go and brew some tea in the kitchen. At least it would keep me busy for a few minutes. I hadn't dared go and sit in the garden for fear of not hearing the doorbell. I'd given up on writing—words eluded me. The only thing left in my head was one single thought.

In a few minutes, I'd be seeing Romaric again.

I filled the kettle and started opening cupboards, taking out the tea, filters, and a spoon. As I set about preparing my favorite drink, I listened to the noise from the street. Was that a car I heard coming up the drive?

When the water came to a boil, I poured water from the kettle into my cup. I stirred the teabag as I relived for the thousandth time in the past three days the moment when Romaric had asked if he could come see me . . .

Saying that leaving Port-l'Abbé had been difficult was probably the understatement of the century.

It had been much worse. I had felt torn apart, as though I were leaving half of myself behind with Rom.

According to my GPS, I'd driven exactly 2.54 kilometers, that is, the distance between the bed-and-breakfast and the exit sign for Port-l'Abbé, before I'd pulled up and collapsed over the steering wheel, sobbing.

I'd waited for my crying fit to pass, the tears to subside, and my breath to stop hitching, then I'd started driving again, feeling that each kilometer taking me farther away from him was an additional needle piercing my heart.

Once in Karouac, I'd gone straight to my father, even before returning home. My two-hour drive—made longer not because I went sightseeing this time, but because I'd had to stop a couple of times, or maybe three or four, to have another crying jag—had left me empty, exhausted, and I was in urgent need of comfort. My father, being the amazing person he was, had immediately understood that something was wrong. My puffy red eyes and disheveled state were probably good clues.

"What's wrong, sweetheart?" he'd asked when I got out of the car.

In spite of all my resolve to be strong and hold up as well as I could—though really, who did I think I was fooling?—I'd collapsed into his arms at once.

"Oh, Papa," I sobbed. "I think I'm in love!"

He'd smiled and stroked my hair tenderly as he hugged me close. "Come in. We'll have some tea and you'll tell me every-thing."

A few moments later, sipping some of my favorite chai tea, I'd given him the expunged version of my week in Port-l'Abbé. I'd told him about Erwan and Romaric, about how the Ker-marrec family had reacted to the letter, about the party, the castle, and the fact that I had fallen in love over the course of just a few days.

"Which is just plain stupid, I know," I added, anticipating his comment.

But his answer hadn't been what I expected.

"You know, sweetheart, I fell in love with your mother in a few hours. A week later, I begged her to become my wife.

Sometimes it's not a matter of time. I'm not saying this is the same with you, and I don't know this young man, but from what you're saying, he seems to return your feelings. Did he say or do anything that would make you think otherwise?"

I shook my head. Quite the contrary, in fact.

"So why are you crying? You have your whole life ahead of you. I'm sure you can find a way to solve the distance problem!"

"I don't know, Papa. I'm afraid. Afraid that in spite of our wanting this with all our hearts, we can't make it work. Afraid that our different ways of life will keep us apart and we will never see each other again. And . . ." I closed my eyes, trying to hold back the tears trying to escape again. "I just miss him so much already!" The words burst out of me, filled with misery.

"And he probably misses you too, honey. But you're going to find a way, I'm sure of it. Just take your time, and trust him. You could be surprised."

I gave him a tremulous smile. "You're right. I'm sorry. It's stupid to get so worked up, it's like I'm a little kid again."

"Not a kid, a woman who just fell in love."

"How am I going to get by without him, Papa?"

"One day at a time, sweetheart. You'll see—before you know it, you two will be together again."

"Maybe. No, you're right, I have to believe. How could he believe in us if I fall apart and start doubting so soon? I love you, Papa," I added, throwing my arms around him and holding him tight. "I don't know what I'd do without you."

All my life, my father has given me good advice. He's been the voice of reason in all things. It was no lie when I said I didn't know what I'd do without him. He'd been my rock, my port in a storm when my mother left, and even now, at almost thirty years old, I still looked to him whenever something was wrong or needed fixing. He could no longer mend my skinned knees with magic kisses, but his presence, his comfort, and his advice were as important to me as ever.

"Go on, go call him," he told me. "I'm sure he's waiting."

I'd called Romaric a few minutes later, sitting in a lawn chair in my father's garden. He'd picked up on the first ring.

"Flavie! I was so worried! Any longer and I would have been the one calling you!"

It felt so good to hear his voice. I could swear I had been gone for days even though it had only been . . . four hours and twelve minutes, my watch informed me. But I missed him already. I missed him so much.

No, Flavie, I told myself. No more crying. You're done now.

"*Sorry.*" *I cleared my throat.* "*The drive was a bit longer than I'd anticipated.*"

"*Did you have an accident? Are you all right?*"

"*No accident, I'm fine. I just made a couple more pit stops than I'd intended to. But I'm just fine, I'm at my father's place.*"

"*Flavie . . .*"

I heard Gwenn calling for him on his end. Rom swore softly, but not softly enough that I would miss it.

"*Listen, can I call you back later? Some customers just got here and they look . . . demanding. Gwenn really needs a hand.*"

"*Okay, call me when you can.*"

"*Tonight. I . . .*" *He hesitated.* "*Tonight,*" *he repeated.* "*I'll call you. I miss you.*"

"*Me too. I'll be waiting.*"

He'd kept his promise and called back later that night.

The next day, after agreeing to an emergency meeting with the girls, I'd sat on my favorite corner of the beach, the one that tourists rarely bothered with because it was hard to reach, and I'd watched the sunset while I thought of Rom. That was when he had called, as though he could read my thoughts. We'd chatted for over an hour. He'd told me about the new customers, a family of five who had very specific ideas as to how their horses should be groomed.

He'd also met Dan, Gwenn's boyfriend, just before he'd called me—both of them had asked Rom to say hello on their behalf. It seemed Erwan was right—Dan was nice and friendly. We'd exchanged a few more meaningless pleasantries just to keep talking, in order not to have to hang up yet.

Then Rom had sighed, and I had braced myself for what was to come.

"*Flavie?*"

"*Mmm?*"

"*I miss you already. I know it's kind of stupid because*

you've only been gone a day, but I can't help it. I miss you. This place feels empty without you."

My heart soared with relief. For a second, I'd been worried he would tell me that our little romp had been fun but it stopped here. I knew that the likelihood was low, given how he had been behaving over the last two days, but I wasn't being completely rational, and I was very, very afraid I'd never see him again.

"So do I, Rom," I'd said. "I miss you too."

I could almost hear him smiling.

"Flavie?"

"Yeah?"

"Can I come and see you?"

YES! I'd felt like screaming into the phone. Come now, straightaway, don't wait, I need you, want you.

Of course, I had said none of that.

"Whenever you want. But . . . What about your place? I thought—"

"I'll work something out. I need to see you, even if it's only for a few hours. I don't know when I'll come yet, but I'll find a way. That's a promise."

I'd hung up with a silly smile on my face.

Parents are always right, it seems.

We'd worked out a routine. Romaric called me every night without fail, and we talked for an hour at least, often more. We shared small pieces of our daily lives and got to know each other better. He kept me updated on the bed-and-breakfast, Gwenn, Erwan, Dan, Moonlight, and Belle; I told him all about my father's birthday, what we did together to take his mind off things, his shop, my knitting circle. He asked me whether I was writing anything. I wasn't—my mind was still too full of him for me to focus on anything else. I asked him whether he had carved anything recently, but he hadn't, and he didn't elaborate on the topic.

Then a few days ago, he'd asked me the question.

"Flavie, can I come over this weekend?"

A knock on the door startled me out of my daydream.

I froze, my entire body shutting down before it rebooted in

earnest. My heart beat double time, blood rushed to my face. It had to be him. I ran to the door and flung it wide open.

There he was, the ground-shaking smile I loved so much on his lips.

"Hi," he said, meeting my eyes. "I sell vacuum cleaners. Can I interest you in buying one?"

I laughed and threw myself into his arms.

Chapter 20

Gwenn by his side, Erwan stopped in the church entrance. Unlike the rest of the town, nothing here had changed. It looked just the same as he remembered it. He turned around, his gaze sliding to the spot where he'd stood forty years ago on Amélie's wedding day, hidden behind the porch at the corner of the street. It was an eternity ago, almost half a lifetime. And yet it seemed as though it was yesterday that he had watched her ascend the steps arm in arm with her father, glowing and ready to marry another man.

He closed his eyes and took a deep breath, as much to calm his beating heart as to brush off the memories assailing him. This pilgrimage to all the places that he'd come to love during his stay in Karouac was to bolster his courage and strength, not to relive painful memories. Those weren't the ones he wanted to remember today.

But just in case, he'd wait a little longer before he went down to the beach.

"Are you okay, Erwan?" Gwenn asked.

"I'm all right. It feels strange to be here after so long."

"I can only imagine. Do you want to go into the church straight-away or wait a little first?"

"Let's go," he said.

"All right." She slipped her arm through his. "Lead on."

Together, they climbed the steps, and Erwan pushed open the heavy wooden door, just as he had done on the last day of summer in 1971.

Other memories flooded him, debates with Father François, long hours spent working on the church, laughter and jokes tossed around. For an instant, he was twenty years old again, living like there was no tomorrow.

"This is nice," Gwenn murmured, letting go of this arm to venture farther inside. "It's light and warm, unlike the churches you usually find all over the place, all cold and dark. I like it. You did good work here."

"You make it sound like I built the church! I just repaired a few sections back there. Here"—he pointed to a wall—"and here. But I agree with you. This church is one of a kind, and I always enjoyed coming here. I would find peace and comfort when I needed to."

"That's kind of funny," Gwenn said, crinkling up her nose.

"Why do you say that?"

"Well, you've always been pretty much an atheist, so it's funny you would come here for peace and comfort. And you worked here. It's like napping in your office."

"I usually worked outside, so it did make a difference. And it wasn't about the religious aspect of things. I didn't come here to pray or talk to God. I came for the silence. There was something here I found soothing. And I liked talking to the parish priest."

"The one Flavie met?"

"Mm-hmm."

They'd reached the center of the transept. Erwan looked around for his statue and soon found it.

"It was such a long time ago." He stepped closer. "I had forgotten . . ." *I had forgotten how much it looks like Amélie.*

"So that's the Virgin Mary statue Flavie was talking about?"

"That's the one."

"It's beautiful. I can't believe you carved it when you were only twenty. You're a genius, uncle mine!" She kissed his cheek. "I'm proud to be your niece, you know."

"Thank you, sweetheart."

"Do my eyes deceive me?" a voice interrupted. "Is this young Erwan? Have you come to make sure I kept my promise to look after the statue you gave me?"

Erwan turned, a smile upon his lips. "Not that young anymore, Father. And I never doubted you would keep your end of the bargain. How are you doing?"

"You'll always be young Erwan to me, I'm afraid." The priest embraced him. "I'm doing well. It's good to see you again, even after such a long time. I have missed you, you know."

"I missed you too. But I . . . I couldn't come back."

"I know. Flavie told me a little about what happened when she came to see me a few days ago. I'm sorry life has dealt you such a harsh hand."

"Thank you, Father. But it's about to change—I've decided to seize my chance again. Better late than never. Do you remember what you told me the day I left?"

"Every word."

"You said if she was meant to be with me . . ."

". . . the Lord would reunite you, yes. And you replied that you'd rather rely on yourself."

"And that's what I'm going to do, even if forty-five years went by before I could gather the courage to do what I should have done a long time ago. I'm going to find Amélie again."

"I hope it works out the way you want, Erwan."

"Thank you, Father."

"Will you come back and see me before I retire? I'd enjoy a few more conversations like the ones we used to have when we were young."

"You're leaving, Father?"

"You might have noticed I'm not getting any younger myself. It's time for some new blood in our parish."

"When will you leave?"

"Not for a few years yet, don't worry. But I wouldn't want another forty-five years to go by before you came back this way. I won't live that long."

"I promise I'll come back as soon as I've found Amélie."

"I'll hold you to that."

"A promise is a promise."

Gwenn cleared her throat conspicuously.

"Father, let me introduce my niece and adopted daughter, Gwenn."

"A pleasure, Gwenn."

"Likewise, Father." Gwenn shook his hand.

"You look like Erwan."

"You should see my older brother. He's the spitting image of Erwan."

"Speaking of Romaric . . . Father, I have to leave. We have someone we need to surprise. Flavie doesn't know we're here yet," Erwan explained with a smile.

"What a pleasant surprise! I've no doubt she will be very glad to see you."

"I certainly hope so!"

"Goodbye then, my dear Erwan, and may God grant you your heart's desire this time."

"Goodbye, Father."

Romaric and I were talking in the entrance—read: kissing as though the world was about to end—and I was mentally planning a tour of the house that would inevitably end in my bedroom, when someone knocked at the door.

I made an executive decision to ignore the ill-timed guest who dared intrude upon our reunion.

"Aren't you going to answer that?" Romaric said.

"Mmm, no, whoever it is can come back later."

The knocking redoubled.

"Maybe you should check it out," Rom suggested.

"Don't wanna. I have much better things to do right now," I replied, wondering why he was so insistent I open the door. Wasn't he in a hurry to move on to the next stage of our reunion?

Once again, the knocking.

"I really think you should go and see. I promise I'm not going anywhere."

I sighed. "If you insist."

As I made my way to the door, I grumbled that whoever it was, I was going to send them back to where they came from and get right back to what I had been doing, and I didn't care what anyone thought about it.

I opened the door, ready to unleash a heap of cutting remarks at my unwelcome caller, and then—

"Erwan! Gwenn! What—"

Questions could wait, I decided as I threw my arms around them, almost—but not quite—as enthusiastically as I had greeted Rom earlier.

"Flavie!" Gwenn hugged me back. "I'm so glad to see you again!"

"What—How—What about your bed-and-breakfast? Did you close? What's going to happen to the horses?"

"Don't worry, some friends of ours are taking care of them. Won't you invite us in?"

"Of course! Please, come in. I'm just so surprised, I forgot my manners. It's great to see you!"

I stepped aside and turned toward a beaming Rom. "You sly fox—you never said a thing."

"We wanted to surprise you."

"Come on, Flavie, ask us why we're here!" Gwenn begged.

"Okay. Why are you here?"

"Flavie," Erwan began, "we're going to find Amélie, and we want you to come with us."

"Really?"

Erwan nodded. I turned to Rom and Gwenn for confirmation and they both agreed wordlessly. "Oh, Erwan!"

I embraced him.

Again.

I really was starting to make a habit of it.

Over the next few hours, we laid out our battle plan. Erwan told us what he wanted to do, I suggested a few changes. Romaric and Gwenn each took part in their own manner: Rom said nothing and Gwenn pointed out a few weaknesses in the plan. The four of us eventually built a solid plan. The only unknown was Amélie. I would have to call her to tell her about the letter without giving away too many details, and convince her to meet with me so I could hand it over.

In the end, we decided to move ahead that very evening. Around 7 p.m.—a time at which I estimated Amélie should be home from work—I sat at my kitchen table, surrounded by Rom, Erwan, and Gwenn, and dialed the number Chantale had given me a lifetime ago.

"It's ringing," I mouthed to the others.

My hands were clammy. I could barely believe I was finally going to speak with Amélie. How many times had I pictured this talk? How many times had I imagined myself calling to share what I had discovered and tell her about Erwan?

"Hello?"

"Ms. Lacombe?" I prayed I wasn't stepping out of line calling her by her maiden name.

"This is she."

"Good evening, ma'am. My name is Flavie Richalet."

"Good evening."

"I apologize for the inconvenience. One of your old friends gave me your number, Chantale Dumas—or, well, actually, it was her older sister, France."

"I know them both quite well. But if I may, why were you trying to reach me?"

"It's sort of a strange story, in fact, but I promise every word is true. You see, I live in Karouac, in what used to be called the principal's house. A few weeks ago, I received a letter addressed to you."

"Oh! How peculiar."

"It is, isn't it? It was sent in the seventies and the post office mislaid it for years. I took the liberty of opening it to see if it was anything important."

"If you're calling me, it must have been," Amélie stated.

"It was."

"What was it?"

"A letter from a friend."

"Who?"

"Uh . . . He didn't sign, so I don't know," I improvised with a grimace.

"All right, it does seem like a strange story. I don't quite know what to say, except perhaps to thank you for letting me know. Could you send it on?"

"To be frank, I'd like to hand it over in person. You see, I'm a historian and I'm planning on writing a novel that takes place in Karouac in the seventies. If I could ask you a few questions, it might help a lot. Would you have a little time to spare? I could kill two birds with one stone."

I crossed my fingers, my toes, anything I could cross as I waited for her answer. *Please let her say yes . . . please let her say yes . . .*

"Well . . . If you want to . . . Why not? But are you really going to come all the way from Karouac just for this?" Amélie asked.

"Um, no, I have to pass through anyway."

I felt a little guilty for telling so many lies and half-truths, and I sincerely hoped she would forgive me when she learned why I had done all this.

"In that case, I'd be willing, yes. It's been a long time since I spoke of Karouac with someone."

"Great! Fantastic! Shall I call you again when I'm there? In a couple of days?"

"Yes, it will be easier to agree on a meeting place then."

"Great! Perfect!" I repeated. "Goodbye then, Ms. Lacombe! I'm so very glad to get to meet you at last."

I hung up, exhilarated.

"She's waiting for us!"

Across the country, in the small town of Valensole, Amélie stared at the phone for several long seconds, frowning.

Who was the slightly crazy person who claimed to have a letter addressed to her? Chantale must trust her if she had given her Amélie's phone number—which was kind of presumptuous on her part, by the way. She could have at least asked permission before handing it out. But still, it was a rather mad story.

Amélie shrugged. She'd know soon enough what it was all about.

Thinking no more about the mysterious call, she returned to her everyday pursuits, unaware that her life was about to change completely.

Chapter 21

Lavender fields stretched out as far as the eye could see. Pale purple flowers filled my line of sight. Somehow, I couldn't get enough of the beauty of this region I was visiting for the first time. I only knew what the internet had told me about the town.

Valensole. The city of lavender.

The end of my journey—of our journey.

Sitting beside me in the back seat, Gwenn pored over a map of the city.

I took a deep breath, inhaling the sweet scent of lavender floating in the air, and my eyes met a sapphire gaze in the rearview mirror. I smiled, and from the crinkles around the corner of his eyes, I knew Rom was smiling back.

"Where will we be staying again, Erwan?" Gwenn asked.

"Route d'Oraison, that's in the northern part of town," Erwan answered from the passenger seat.

"Got it. Not too far from here."

"No, we should be there in twenty minutes."

"Good, I need to stretch my legs!"

I leaned back against the headrest as Erwan and Gwenn talked, and gazed over the surrounding fields, drifting into a daydream.

By some stroke of luck—which I had chosen to interpret as a sign that the stars were aligning in our favor—a last-minute cancellation two days ago had allowed us to book rooms in an adorable little bed-and-breakfast right in the middle of the lavender fields just north of Valensole, rather than in the drab hotel where we had resolved to bunk down after our unsuccessful search for better accommodations. Yes, I know—what else did we expect, trying to book a room with little notice during high tourist season in southern France? But we were on a mission.

The next day—that is, yesterday—we had piled our bags into the trunk of Erwan's car, and with Romaric at the wheel, we hit the road southward. We'd stopped for the night in a little hotel halfway between Karouac and Valensole, and we'd been up at the break of dawn this morning. Our surroundings had turned to lavender fields awhile back, and I simply could not tire of the gorgeous landscape that was so different from the Breton coastline and yet just as magical.

I smiled to myself, and once again my gaze strayed to meet Romaric's in the rearview mirror.

"This is it," he announced. "Valensole."

I sat up. Here we were at last, in the town where Amélie lived. Erwan's fate was going to be decided here.

The town was small and adorable. Most of the buildings were old, made of light-colored stone, and looked like they could have told a hundred stories if they had a voice to speak with. We drove through town to reach the route d'Oraison and leave our bags in the bed-and-breakfast before we could proceed with the next step of our plan.

When we arrived there, we could see that the online brochure had not lied about the beauty of the establishment.

The house was built of pale ochre stone, with a red slate roof and blue window shutters, and it sat right in the middle of a lavender field.

"Wow, this is amazing!" Gwenn exclaimed as she spun around and looked at our surroundings.

I could only agree. Not even the most jaded tourist could have resisted such a view.

The owners were a smiling elderly couple who welcomed us effusively and led us straight to our room—one for me and Rom, and the other that Erwan and Gwenn would share. We agreed to freshen up and meet on the terrace a few minutes later.

Gwenn and Erwan were already waiting when Rom and I came down. I sat between the two men and took out my phone.

"Ready?" I asked Erwan.

He nodded.

"Here we go." My heart was pounding and my hands shook slightly as I dialed Amélie's number.

"Ms. Lacombe? This is Flavie Richalet speaking."

"Hello, Flavie. How are you?"

"Very well, thank you. What about you?" I said politely.

"Just fine, thank you."

"I'm calling to tell you that I've just arrived in Valensole, and if you're available, I'm free for the day."

"Well, I'm off in a couple of hours." She paused. "Why don't we meet up somewhere?"

"I would love that!" I fought to keep the excitement out of my voice.

"Do you know where the town hall is?"

"Yes."

"There's a little park just behind the building, nice and shady. It's very comfortable when the weather is as hot as it is today. Shall we meet there in . . . say . . . two and a half hours?"

"That would be perfect! I'm wearing a pink dress."

"I'm wearing red, and I'll have a notebook in my hand."

"Duly noted! Until later, then," Flavie concluded.

"Precisely."

I waited for her to hang up, then slowly lowered my phone, my eyes on Erwan. "This is it. We're meeting in two and a half hours in the park behind the town hall."

Two hours later, we moved into place. Everything had been set up so we could watch Amélie arrive without giving ourselves away. Or, well, without giving Erwan away. I was to walk up to her first, then discreetly slip away as soon as Erwan showed himself. I was slightly ill at ease with such a setup, but this was for a good cause, so their reunion would be even more wonderful than I hoped it would be. No, I *knew* it would be magical. There simply was no other way. This story could only have a happy ending.

We had rehearsed everything, timed it to the minute. Only one thing was still missing—our guest of honor.

Minutes felt like hours. I could barely imagine what must be going through Erwan's mind and heart. Anxiety. Impatience. Fear. Love.

At last, Amélie appeared around the bend in the path. She strolled closer at a calm, leisurely pace, entirely unaware of what awaited her. She was tall and beautiful. Her gray hair was still streaked with red and she was magnificent, plain and simple. She had the grace of a ballerina, the poise of an aristocrat, the beauty of a goddess. I chanced a quick glance at Erwan, whose eyes were riveted to her, his entire body stock-still, transfixed.

Amélie sat on a bench and opened her handbag, drawing out a small notebook she began to doodle in. I waited a few minutes, until the clock struck half past six, then I stepped out of the shadows and made my way toward her.

"Ms. Lacombe?"

She looked up, taking in my pink dress with her green eyes, and smiled. "Ms. Richalet, I presume?"

"You presume well." I extended a hand. "But please call me Flavie."

"All right. I'm Amélie."

Her grip was gentle but firm. I couldn't believe I was standing in front of her. Just like with Erwan, I had dreamed of this moment for so long that it had become slightly surreal—but so very exciting. In a few minutes, I was going to reunite Erwan and Amélie!

I carefully sat next to her, and she turned toward me, facing away from Erwan, Rom, and Gwenn, whose gazes I could feel upon us.

"Thank you so much for agreeing to meet with me out of the blue. You cannot imagine the lengths I went to in order to find you."

"It must be a very important letter for you to go so far out of your way to return it to me," she commented, eyebrows raised.

"It is."

"Well? What's this about, then?"

"As I told you over the phone, I received a letter addressed to you. It was mailed in 1971."

"It certainly took its sweet time arriving!" Amélie sounded amused.

"It sure did!"

"You're making me curious. Who could have written me back in 1971 who was so important that you'd come all this way to tell me?"

"Someone who loved you very much. Actually, someone who loved you, period. And to tell you the truth . . . he insisted on bringing it himself."

And as I spoke the words, I looked up toward Erwan, who had stepped forward, letter in hand. Amélie turned around and froze. Slowly, she got to her feet.

"Erwan," she breathed.

"Hello, Amélie," he said gently.

I tiptoed away to join Romaric and Gwenn, leaving Erwan and Amélie face-to-face to try to bridge the forty-five year gap that lay between them.

She hasn't changed a bit, Erwan thought, sitting beside her. She was still devastatingly beautiful, and he found himself short of breath the way he had been back then. Four decades had passed, but his love for her was as strong, as deep, and as everlasting as it had always been.

His heart pounded in his chest. He wouldn't have thought that at over sixty years of age, he could still feel the same fear, the same anxiety as he had in his youth. The rest of his life was going to be decided here during the next few minutes, and he was as frightened as a child.

"I didn't expect you," Amélie admitted.

"I know."

She looked astounded. He would have been too, had he been in her place. But she had recognized him at once. That could only mean that she had not forgotten him over the years.

"It's been so long," she ventured.

"Forty-five years."

"Forty-five years," she agreed. "Next month."

Had she counted the years and the months too?

A wave of hope swept over him.

"I waited for you." There was sadness in her voice. Pain, and a hint of reproach too. "You never came."

"I know."

"I got married."

"I know. I was there. You were gorgeous. You looked like a fairy princess in your wedding gown."

She'd always been his princess. His fairy.

"You were there?" She frowned. "But . . ."

"I hid under a porch. I was too late."

Could she feel his pain? Could she guess how much he regretted arriving too late? He would have given anything to go back and erase history, to write a new story for the both of them.

"You didn't keep your promise," she admonished gently. "You didn't write, or come back, even though you had promised to. I suffered because of you. You broke my heart with silence."

"But I did write, Amélie."

He extended the letter.

She gazed down upon it for a long while before she carefully opened the envelope and delicately tugged the letter out, unfolded it, and started to read. Erwan kept silent, taking in the sight of her. For several long seconds, she remained still, her eyes riveted to the paper. A single tear ran down her cheek and she brushed it away.

Then she raised her eyes, and he could read the question in her shimmering gaze.

"You never received it. But Flavie did, a few weeks ago. Far too late."

It's never too late, Flavie's voice whispered in his head.

"You *did* write," Amélie choked out, her throat tight with emotion.

It wasn't a question.

"Yes." Erwan exhaled. "I asked you to marry me. And when you didn't answer, I tried to call you. Your mother came to the phone. She . . . she didn't know who I was. I can't tell you how it hurt that you didn't tell them about me. But I gave her my address and phone number, and pleaded with her to give them to you. And once again, I waited for you to answer, for a long time. A very long time. Too long, in fact, long after it had become too late."

Amélie froze.

"That was you?"

"What do you mean?" Erwan frowned.

"When I came home for Christmas that year, I scrounged up the courage to ask my mother if anyone had called or written. I hadn't lost hope, despite your silence—or, well, what I thought was your silence."

She let out a sigh, her eyes on the ground.

"I know . . . I know I should have told them about you sooner, but . . . communication with them was difficult at that time. That was why I left for Paris. I couldn't stand it anymore. I managed to convince them to let me go to that school, but . . . I knew they wouldn't approve of you being a stonemason, so I didn't say anything."

"You never told me that," Erwan said.

Even after all this time, it still hurt to hear that he would never have been good enough for her parents. But at least now he understood.

"No. I didn't want to spoil what we had. You were my escape, Erwan. My escape from real life. I loved you with all my heart, and I didn't want to hurt you."

She paused and when she started talking again he could feel the regret in her voice.

"I ended up hurting you anyway."

"All that is in the past now. What . . . what did your mother say when you asked if I had called?" he asked, hesitating, afraid of hearing the answer.

"She said that indeed, someone had called, but when she looked for it, she couldn't find the paper where she'd taken down the details. She had always been a bit of a scatterbrain and maybe she had just thrown out the paper without realizing it. She did, however, remember the name quite well."

She paused. Erwan hung on very word, waiting for her to go on.

"Antoine. That's what she told me. I thought that the world was crumbling around me. I had hoped that you were my mysterious caller. I don't think I've ever been so disappointed."

"Antoine," Erwan repeated.

They had been so close to finding each other again! To think that a simple misunderstanding could keep them apart for so many years . . .

He had to wonder what God they had offended in a former life to pay such a price now.

"If I had known it was you—" Amélie began. She stopped and looked down.

"What would you have done, if you had known it was me?" Erwan asked shyly.

"I would have tried to find you," she confessed. "I—I wouldn't have given up so soon." She took a deep breath, as though to brace herself for what she was about to say, and went on without looking at him. "I never tried to find you, Erwan, because I was convinced you had forgotten me. That I was only one of your conquests."

"Never. Not for a minute."

Amélie glanced up, and their eyes met.

"I never forgot you for a single second, Amélie. Even now, there is not a day that passes that I don't think of you, regret I didn't fight harder for you, and that I didn't carry you away from that church and stop you from marrying that man. And if I had known all of this before, if I had had even the slightest inkling that you hadn't received my letter or heard of my phone call, if I had been aware that you were divorced, I would never have waited this long. Believe me, I would have been here on my knees, begging you to forgive me for being such an idiot, for not telling you how much I cared for you, for not showing that you were—that you still are—the woman of my dreams."

Tears spilled from Amélie's eyes.

"You're not the only one at fault here, Erwan," she murmured, never taking her eyes off him. "I have my share of responsibility in this mess. I didn't trust you enough, didn't trust our love. I should have fought harder for you too."

"It's not too late," Erwan said.

He cupped Amélie's face in his hands, gently resting his forehead against hers. "I love you, Amélie. I have loved you since the day we met."

"Me too, Erwan," she whispered. "I love you. I have loved only you. I tried to make myself forget you, I even got married, but I was fooling myself. Nothing could ever erase you from my memory, or from my heart."

Erwan thought his heart would burst out of his chest for joy.

"Then give me another chance, Amélie. Give us a chance to be happy again."

Erwan and Amélie talked for a long time. I curled up in Romaric's embrace, his hand gently stroking my arm, and kept an eye on them. The longer the conversation carried on, the more relaxed Amélie became, tension flowing out of her body. She shifted imperceptibly closer to Erwan, and I saw a tear roll down her cheek when she finally read the letter, forty-five years after it had been meant to reach her. *So many years lost and wasted*, I thought then.

But the past is in the past, and it cannot be changed. We can only do our best so our future holds no regrets.

After what felt like an eternity, I saw Erwan reach out to cradle Amélie's face between his hands and bring their foreheads together—a gesture he had in common with Romaric. He said something, Amélie whispered something back, and it was as though the sun lit Erwan up from inside. He kissed her slowly, gently, reverently, as though she were the most precious thing in the universe. I turned my gaze away, trying to preserve their intimacy. This moment was for them, and them alone.

A few more minutes went by before Amélie and Erwan came over to join us, hand in hand.

We rose as they drew closer.

"Romaric, Gwenn, I'd like to introduce you to somebody," Erwan said shyly. He turned to Amélie and went on. "Amélie, these are Gwenn and Romaric, my niece and nephew and adopted children. And you already know Flavie. Rom, Gwenn . . . this is Amélie. My Amélie."

"Erwan, I'm so happy for you both!" I exclaimed as I hugged him. "After all these twists and turns, fate finally brought you back together!"

"Well, you gave fate a bit of a nudge," Gwenn teased me, elbowing me gently. "Amélie, I'm so glad to meet you at last," she added, embracing her.

"Thank you! I'm very glad to meet you too. And . . . thank you for bringing Erwan back to me," she said as she turned to me and embraced me.

I hugged her back. "You're welcome," I murmured. "You're very welcome."

And as I watched Erwan and Amélie take turns hugging Gwenn and Romaric, their faces radiant with joy, a thought crept unbidden across my mind. My father had been right—nothing is forever, and you should never give up.

Erwan and Amélie were living proof of this.

"You were right," Romaric told me that evening as we walked hand in hand through the lavender fields.

We'd left Erwan at Amélie's place after dinner, aware that they still had many things to share and that they probably didn't want "the children" hanging around while they talked. Amélie had invited us over, and time had simply flown by in a whirlwind of laughter, jokes, and stories. For once I had listened rather than participated in the conversation. I had held myself a little apart, watching as a family came together, and I realized that Chantale was right. Amélie was a wonderful person. She was kind and considerate, and truly interested in other people. Despite being over sixty, she was stunningly beautiful, and young at heart. I had loved listening to her speak of her fashion line and her creations. She had blushed when admitting that my intuition was right—the K in her designer brand did stand for Kermarrec.

"But officially, I told everyone it was a reference to the town I came from," she had explained.

She'd told us about the life she'd lived for over forty years, about the amazing experiences she'd had, detailing her trip around the world after her divorce, to find herself again. And judging from the looks Erwan had given her, I hadn't been the only one enthralled by her stories.

Amélie was also an excellent cook; she hadn't had much difficulty in convincing us to stay for dinner. She'd firmly turned down offers to help and disappeared into her kitchen, and in no time at all, she'd whipped up a delicious meal, complete with a mouthwatering dessert, and even unearthed a bottle of rosé to go with the food.

As soon as the last drop of coffee had disappeared and the last dish had been washed, Gwenn and I shared a look and, suspecting that they still had a lot to catch up on suggested Erwan stay at Amélie's while we went back to the bed-and-breakfast, offering to come and pick him up in the morning. He'd accepted, and I couldn't help but find the light blush spreading over his cheeks endearing. After all these years, Erwan still had some of his natural shyness.

We had left them to their privacy and returned to the bed-and-breakfast. Gwenn had shut herself in her room to call her boyfriend while Rom and I went for a walk.

"It happens fairly often," I told him with exaggerated smugness. "I'm a teacher, it's an occupational hazard. What exactly was I right about, this time?"

I trailed a hand through the lavender bushes, then raised it to my face, inhaling the sweet scent that clung to my skin.

"It would have been a mistake not to come."

I kept silent. I knew it had been a hard road for Rom and that he had needed some time to acknowledge the fact that this was the best thing for Erwan.

"I've never seen him so happy," he added.

"All's well that ends well." I sighed.

"Not quite."

He stopped in his tracks and turned to face me. "There's something we should talk about."

My heart started pounding like a drum. "Yes?" I squeaked, trying to mask the fear that lurked in my gut.

"I know that what we have is still very new. That we haven't been seeing each other for long, that it's too early yet to make plans. We should take our time. But—"

He paused, and my breath came a little easier. Just a tad, mind you. "But?"

"Flavie, I'm in love with you. I'm in love with your smile, with your eyes, with the kindness you show to those around you. I'm in love with your humor, with your joie de vivre, your enthusiasm, your insatiable curiosity. I'm in love with your body, with your lips. I love you. I don't know what we can do yet, but I do know that the last two weeks without you have been unbearable, empty and gray. The days were bleak because you weren't there. I missed you, Flavie, I missed you so much! More than I can say. I know this is moving too fast, that it's probably too early for you, but—"

"No."

"No . . . what?"

"No, it's not too early for me. I love you, Romaric, and believe me, the last couple of weeks were just as long and dreary for me as they were for you. I love you—I think I fell in love at first sight, the first time the earth shook under my feet. And nothing could make me happier than building a life with you, whatever it may be."

A smile broke like sunrise across his face, and right there, in the midst of the lavender fields, he kissed me as though I had just offered him the moon.

But in truth, I had been the one graced with a gift.

Once again, my father had been right.

You just need to have faith.

Epilogue

Karouac, Brittany
A year later

"Ladies and gentlemen, we are gathered here today to celebrate the union of two souls in holy matrimony."

Father François's voice rang out into the church. He smiled at the assembly, and I smiled back.

It was the most wonderful day of my life.

Or, at least, the second most wonderful. The top spot belonged to the day I had married Romaric.

My gaze slid over my left ring finger and the stunning diamond that graced it. When Romaric had knelt down on the beach in Karouac at sunset a few months ago, and asked me to become his wife, proffering his mother's engagement ring, I had braced myself to wake up any moment. I'd pinched myself just to be sure I wasn't dreaming. My very own Prince Charming was asking me to make an honest man of him and become the mother of his children—and his horses.

We married a few weeks later in a small ceremony. Only our closest friends had been invited—including, naturally, Erwan, Amélie, and her two daughters, who had come down from Paris just for the occasion, and Gwenn and Dan, her mysterious partner from the ball. Of course, in the meantime he had lost most of his mystery and become more or less a part of the family as interim owner of the bed-and-breakfast. Rom had handed it over to him while we waited for me to be transferred to southern Brittany so we could move back to Port-l'Abbé.

I had dithered for some time over the idea of leaving my father behind—as well as relinquishing my house, I admit—but we'd talked it over at length and we'd come to a compromise. My father had promised to close the shop for a few weeks in July and come spend some time with me. If he hadn't, he knew as well as I did that my decision would have been much harder to make.

In the end, after much hemming and hawing, I had decided to keep my house. Six years ago I couldn't stand the idea that someone else might live in it, which had prompted me to buy it. I could bear the idea even less now I had lived in it. It was too important to me, to us. I'd called a family meeting with my father, Erwan and Amélie, Gwenn and Dan, and Rom and me, and together we'd decided that it had to stay in the family. Rom and I would pop in during the school holidays and low tourist season to visit my father and the knitting circle without having to trespass on anyone's hospitality, and the rest of the year, it would be available to anyone who wanted to relax away from the busy crowds of tourists. We could even rent it to tourists, if need be. It was an ideal compromise for everyone. I hadn't even had to bring up the money side of the equation—always a sensitive topic—before Gwenn, Amélie, and Erwan had spontaneously offered to chip in so we could all share the upkeep costs.

I really had the best family in the world.

"Erwan Alban Patrick Kermarrec, do you take Amélie Virginie Sophie Lacombe for your wife, to love her and cherish her, for better or for worse, until death do you part?"

Erwan gazed intently into Amélie's eyes and he intoned clearly, "I do."

The priest smiled.

So did I.

"And do you, Amélie Virginie Sophie Lacombe, take Erwan Alban Patrick Kermarrec for your husband, to love him and cherish him, for better or for worse, until death do you part?"

Amélie's response was as clear and determined as Erwan's. "I do."

"You are now married in the eyes of God."

I brushed a tear away. Weddings made me so emotional. I slid a glance toward Romaric, who saw I was about to burst out sobbing any minute and curled an arm around my shoulders, drawing me into a protective embrace. He dropped a tender kiss on my hair and hugged me, a mischievous smile playing around his lips. But try as he might to seem unaffected, I knew he was as moved as I was.

Today his uncle, the man who had been his father in all but name for most of his life, was getting married to his one and true love. After waiting for all these years, Erwan was at long last going to have the life he deserved with the woman he loved. And nothing could make Rom happier than seeing Erwan alight with joy in the church that had been such a fundamental part of his life.

Even though it had taken a few discreet conversations with Father François to achieve this—Amélie was, after all, divorced.

The priest blessed the rings, and Amélie and Erwan turned to face each other.

"Amélie, I give you this ring as a symbol of our love and fidelity," Erwan said softly as he slipped the band onto a glowing Amélie's finger.

"Erwan, I give you this ring as a symbol of our love and fidelity," she murmured back.

"I now pronounce you husband and wife." Father François beamed. "You may kiss the bride."

And in front of the whole assembly, Erwan reached out to cradle Amélie's face gently in his hands and gave her what had to be the sweetest kiss in history, brimming with restrained passion yet exquisitely moving. I even caught a glimpse of a tear rolling down his face.

It had taken them forty-five years to find each other.

Forty-five years to overcome the obstacles in their path.

But they had succeeded, and now nothing could ever stop them from being happy again.

And the novel, you ask. Did I write it?

I did. Under the gentle pressure of my friends from the knitting circle, who had refused to take no for an answer, I submitted it to my publisher. My editor loved it, and so it had been published.

Against all expectations, my novel became a best seller, and I had kept two of my author's copies, discreetly slipping them onto the table bearing the presents for the happy couple.

It would be my wedding gift—the story of their love.

What about the title, might you ask? Had I called it *The Letter Came on a Tuesday*, as I implied at the beginning of the story?

No. In the end, I had chosen another title, a better-fitting one.

I had called it *Stolen Time*.

Acknowledgments

Writing is generally considered to be solitary work, and this is true most of the time. But this book would never have been published if not for the support and assistance of several people, and I would like to thank them all.

To Carine, Caroline, and Cécile, my best friends, and to Vanessa, my little sister, for their unyielding support even—and especially—when I doubted myself, and for reading the first draft when it was still far from perfect.

To Shelbylee, for regaling me with stories from her life as a teacher and opening the door to her world for the span of a novel.

To Suzanne, for everything, plain and simple.

To my very own Prince Charming, for supporting me and putting up with me all through the writing and proofreading of this novel, for believing in me the way he does, and for making my life into a never-ending fairy tale.

This story would never be what it is without my French editor's amazing work. Thank you, Marie, for all the hours, for all your advice, and for always taking me one step further, even when I thought I had reached my limits.

Many thanks to Domitille, for her skillful translation of my words. And a huge thank-you to Tara, my wonderful American editor, who took a leap of faith with Flavie and gave me much precious advice as I worked on the editing. I thank you, from the bottom of my heart.

And of course, a book would be nothing without readers, so many thanks to all of you for trusting me enough to buy this book. I hope you enjoyed reading it as much I did writing it.

As a small girl, **Chloé Duval** used to fill her notebooks with stories about knights fighting terrifying dragons to save damsels in distress. She may have grown up, but her stories still retain a touch of the sweetness and enchantment of her childhood fairy tales.

Though born in France, she considers Canada to be her second home. She lives in Montréal with her Prince Charming and several dozen of her characters.